JOAN DIDION was born in California and lives in ...
City. She is the author of five novels and eight books of
non-fiction, including the international bestseller *The Year
of Magical Thinking*, which was also adapted into a play. Her
most recent book is a second memoir, *Blue Nights*.

From the reviews of *The Last Thing He Wanted*:

'A gripping story . . . Didion's most uncomfortable and bril-
liant book yet'   EMMA TENNANT, *Observer*

'Didion's language is as high-toned as it is hip, an amalgam
of journalistic and political jargons with pared-down prose
full of finely sprung rhythms, suggestive pauses and patterns
of repetition and variation as artful and shapely as song'
                    LUCY HUGHES-HALLETT, *Sunday Times*

'Anyone who is interested in serious writing should read
everything Joan Didion writes. She would be on any short-
list of major contemporary American writers'
                    GEORGE DEMPSEY, *Sunday Independent*

'Marvelous notation of disaffection and despair . . . where
dark detail, understatement and intelligence work their
astonishing magic'   MICHAEL WOOD, *New York Times*

'An impressive, fast-talking, hard-boiled, wise-cracking,
tough-guy of a novel'   PHILIP HENSHER, *Mail on Sunday*

'Fast-paced, witty, inventive . . . *The Last Thing He Wanted*
is a creation of high seriousness, a thriller composed with
all the resources of a unique gift for imaginative literature'
                    ELIZABETH HARDWICK, *New York Review of Books*

'The centrality of *The Last Thing He Wanted* is not a person, nor even an event, but the *tone* of the US in 1984. The technique of writing is, as usual, unique, an incantation with repetitions and rhythms to entrance the reader, meant to restore full weight to a language made weightless by misuse . . . I should perhaps also mention that I read it twice for pure delight before reading it for review'

VERONICA HORWELL, *Guardian*

'[A] tersely beautiful work . . . Her narrator may be classified as paranoid, but her fear is justified: its fruit is ecstatic communion with the reader, and with the landscapes she passes through. What thrills in *The Last Thing He Wanted* is not the plot but the slow disintegration of the protagonist's self . . . Didion gives a definitive portrait of existence on the margins of permanent address'

WAYNE KOESTENBAUM, *London Review of Books*

'[A] terrific story'

MICHAEL KERRIGAN, *Times Literary Supplement*

'A masterful, imaginative yet impeccably well controlled literary thriller . . . Didion, one of America's finest writers . . . demonstrates, again, her career-long fascination with American politics and the American psychosis. She is revered for style as much as for story-telling, but *The Last Thing He Wanted* shows how respect for narrative is indispensable even for a style queen'

MICHAEL THOMPSON-NOEL, *Financial Times*

JOAN DIDION

The Last Thing He Wanted

FOURTH ESTATE • *London*

Fourth Estate
An imprint of HarperCollins*Publishers*
1 London Bridge Street,
London SE1 9GF

This Fourth Estate paperback edition published 2011

First published in Great Britain by Flamingo in 1997

Copyright © Joan Didion 1996

Joan Didion asserts the moral right to be identified as the author of this work

A catalogue record for this book is available from the British Library

ISBN 978-0-00-745424-2

Set in Sabon

Printed and bound by CPI Group (UK) Ltd, Croydon, CR0 4YY

MIX
Paper from
responsible sources
FSC
www.fsc.org   **FSC C007454**

Grateful acknowledgement is made to the following for permission to reprint previously published material:

Liveright Publishing Corporation: Excerpts from 'Voyages II' from *Complete Poems of Hart Crane*, edited by Marc Simon, copyright © 1933, 1958, 1966 by Liveright Publishing Corporation, copyright © 1986 by Marc Simon. Reprinted by permission of Liveright Publishing Corporation.

MCA Music Publishing and Jay Livingston Music: Excerpt from 'Bonanza', words and music by Ray Evans and Jay Livingston, copyright © 1959 by St Angelo Music and Jay Livingston Music, copyright renewed. All rights for St Angelo Music controlled and administered by MCA Music Publishing, a division of MCA, Inc. International copyright secured. All rights reserved. Reprinted by permission of MCA Music Publishing, a division of MCA, Inc., and Jay Livingston Music.

The Last Thing
He Wanted

This book is for Quintana
and for John.

One

I

Some real things have happened lately. For a while we felt rich and then we didn't. For a while we thought time was money, find the time and the money comes with it. Make money for example by flying the Concorde. Moving fast. Get the big suite, the multi-line telephones, get room service on one, get the valet on two, premium service, out by nine back by one. Download all data. Uplink Prague, get some conference calls going. Sell Allied Signal, buy Cypress Minerals, work the management plays. Plug into this news cycle, get the wires raw, nod out on the noise. *Get me audio*, someone was always saying in the nod where we were. *Agence Presse is moving this story*. Somewhere in the nod we were dropping cargo. Somewhere in the nod we were losing infrastructure, losing redundant systems, losing specific gravity. Weightlessness seemed at the time the safer mode. Weightlessness seemed at the time the mode in which we could beat both the clock and affect itself, but I see now that it was not. I see now that the clock was ticking. I see now that we were experiencing not weightlessness but what is interestingly described on page 1513 of the

3

Merck Manual (Fifteenth Edition) as a sustained reactive depression, a bereavement reaction to the leaving of familiar environments. I see now that the environment we were leaving was that of feeling rich. I see now that there will be no Resolution Trust to do the workout on this particular default, but I did not see it then.

Not that I shouldn't have.

There were hints all along, clues we should have registered, processed, sifted for their application to the general condition. Try the day we noticed that the banks had called in the paper on all the malls, try the day we noticed that somebody had called in the paper on all the banks. Try the day we noticed that when we pressed 800 to do some business in Los Angeles or New York we were no longer talking to Los Angeles or New York but to Orlando or Tucson or Greensboro, North Carolina. Try the day we noticed (this will touch a nerve with frequent fliers) the new necessity for changes of equipment at Denver, Raleigh-Durham, St. Louis. Try, as long as we are changing equipment in St. Louis, the unfinished but already bankrupt Gateway Airport Tower there, its boutiques boarded up, its oyster bar shuttered, no more terrycloth robes in the empty cabanas and no more amenity kits in the not quite terrazzo bathrooms: this should have alerted us, should have been processed, but we were moving fast. We were traveling light. We were younger. So was she.

2

For the record this is me talking.
You know me, or think you do.
The not quite omniscient author.
No longer moving fast.
No longer traveling light.

When I resolved in 1994 to finally tell this story, register the clues I had missed ten years before, process the information before it vanished altogether, I considered reinventing myself as PAO at the embassy in question, a career foreign service officer operating under the USICA umbrella. "Lilianne Owen" was my name in that construct, a strategy I ultimately jettisoned as limiting, small-scale, an artifice to no point. *She told me later,* Lilianne Owen would have had to keep saying, and *I learned this after the fact.* As Lilianne Owen I was unconvincing even to myself. As Lilianne Owen I could not have told you half of what I knew.

I wanted to come at this straight.

I wanted to bring my own baggage and unpack it in front of you.

When I first heard this story there were elements

that seemed to me questionable, details I did not trust. The facts of Elena McMahon's life did not quite hang together. They lacked coherence. Logical connections were missing, cause and effect. I wanted the connections to materialize for you as they eventually did for me. The best story I ever told was a reef dream. This is something different.

The first time Treat Morrison ever saw Elena McMahon she was sitting alone in the coffee shop at the Intercon. He had flown down from Washington on the American that landed at ten a.m. and the embassy driver had dropped him at the Intercon to leave his bag and there was this American woman, he did not think a reporter (he knew most of the reporters who covered this part of the world, the reporters stayed close to where they believed the story was, that was the beauty of operating on an island where the story had not yet appeared on the screen), an American woman wearing a white dress and reading the classified page of the local paper and sitting alone at a round table set for eight. Something about this woman had bothered him. In the first place he did not know what she was doing there. He had known she was an American because he recognized in her voice when she spoke to a waiter the slight flat drawl of the American Southwest, but the American women left on the island were embassy or the very occasional reporter, and neither would be sitting at apparent loose ends in the Intercon coffee shop. In the second place this American woman was eating, very slowly and methodically, first a bite of one and then a bite of the other, a chocolate parfait and bacon. The chocolate parfait and bacon had definitely bothered him.

At the time Treat Morrison saw Elena McMahon eating the parfait and bacon in the coffee shop at the Intercon she had been staying not at the Intercon but out on the windward side of the island, in two adjoining rooms with an efficiency kitchen at a place called the Surfrider. When she first came to the Surfrider, in July of that summer, it had been as assistant manager, hired to be in charge of booking return flights and baby-sitters and day tours (the sugar mill plus the harbor plus the island's single Palladian Revival great house) for the young Canadian families who had until recently favored the place because it was cheap and because its Olympic-length pool was deeper at no point than three feet. She had been introduced to the manager of the Surfrider by the man who ran the car-rental agency at the Intercon. Experience in the travel industry was mandatory, the manager of the Surfrider had said, and she had faked it, faked the story and the supporting letters of reference about the three years as social director on the Swedish cruise ship later reflagged (this was the inspired invention, the detail that rendered the references uncheckable) by Robert Vesco. At the time she was hired the island was still getting occasional misguided tourists, not rich tourists, not the kind who required villas with swimming pools and pink sand beaches and butlers and laundresses and multiple telephone lines and fax machines and instant access to Federal Express, but tourists nonetheless, mostly depressed young American couples with backpacks and retired day-trippers from the occasional cruise ship that still put in: those less acutely able to consider time so valuable that they would spend it only in the world's most perfect places. After the first State Department advisory the cruise ships had stopped, and after the second and more urgent advisory a week later (which coincided with the baggage handlers' strike and the withdrawal of two of the four international air carriers with routes to the island) even the backpackers had migrated to less demonstrably imperfect destinations. The Surfrider's Olympic-length pool had been drained. Whatever need there had been for an assistant manager had contracted, then evaporated. Elena McMahon had pointed this out to the manager but he had reasonably suggested that since her rooms would be empty in any case she might just as well stay on, and she had. She liked the place empty. She liked the way the shutters had started losing their slats. She liked the low clouds, the glitter on the sea, the pervasive smell of mildew and bananas. She liked to walk up the road from the parking lot and hear the voices from the Pentecostal church there. She liked to stand on the beach in front of the hotel and know that there was no solid land between her and Africa. "Tourism—Recolonialization by Any Other Name?" was the wishful topic at the noon brown-bag AID symposium the day Treat Morrison arrived at the embassy.

3

If you remember 1984, which I notice fewer and fewer of us care to do, you already know some of what happened to Elena McMahon that summer. You know the context, you remember the names, *Theodore Shackley Clair George Dewey Clarridge Richard Secord Alan Fiers Felix Rodriguez aka "Max Gomez" John Hull Southern Air Lake Resources Stanford Technology Donald Gregg Aguacate Elliott Abrams Robert Owen aka "T.C." Ilopango aka "Cincinnati,"* all swimming together in the glare off the C-123 that fell from the sky into Nicaragua. Not many women got caught in this glare. There was one, the blonde, the shredder, the one who transposed the numbers of the account at the Credit Suisse (the account at the Credit Suisse into which the Sultan of Brunei was to transfer the ten million dollars, in case you have forgotten the minor plays), but she had only a bit part, day work, a broadly comic but not in the end a featured role.

Elena McMahon was different.

Elena McMahon got caught, but not in the glare.

If you wanted to see how she got caught you would probably begin with the documents.

There are documents, more than you might think.

Depositions, testimony, cable traffic, some of it not yet declassified but much in the public record.

You could pick up a thread or two in the usual libraries: Congress of course. The Foreign Policy Institute at Hopkins, the Center for Strategic and International Studies at Georgetown. The Sterling at Yale for the Brokaw correspondence. The Bancroft at Berkeley, where Treat Morrison's papers went after his death.

There are the FBI interviews, none what I would call illuminating but each offering the occasional moment (the chocolate parfait and bacon is one such moment in the transcripts of the FBI interviews), the leading detail (I found it suggestive that the subject who mentioned the parfait and bacon to the FBI was not in fact Treat Morrison), the evasion so blatant that it inadvertently billboards the very fact meant to be obscured.

There are the published transcripts of the hearings before the select committee, ten volumes, two thousand five hundred and seven pages, sixty-three days of testimony arresting not only for its reliance on hydraulic imagery (there were the conduits, there was the pipeline, there was of course the diversion) but for its collateral glimpses of life on the far frontiers of the Monroe Doctrine. There was for example the airline that operated out of St. Lucia but had its headquarters in Frankfurt (Volume VII, Chapter 4, "Implementing the Decision to Take Policy Underground") and either was or was not (conflicting testimony on this) ninety-nine percent owned by a former Air West flight attendant who either did or did not live on St. Lucia. There was for example the team of unidentified men (Volume X, Chapter 2, "Supplemental Material on the Diversion") who either did or did not (more conflicting testimony) arrive on the northern Costa Rican border to burn the bodies of the crew of the unmarked DC-3 that at the time it crashed appeared to be registered to the airline that was or was not ninety-nine percent owned by the former Sky West flight attendant who did or did not live on St. Lucia.

There is of course newspaper coverage, much of it less than fruitful: although a comprehensive database search on *McMahon, Elena* will yield, for the year in question, upwards of six hundred references in almost as many newspapers, all but a handful of them lead to the same two AP stories.

History's rough draft.

We used to say.

When we still believed that history merited a second look.

Not that this was a situation about which many people would have been willing to talk for attribution, or even on background. As someone who quite accidentally happened to be present at the embassy in question at the time in question, I myself refused a dozen or so press requests for interviews. At the time, I chose to believe that I refused such requests because they seemed to impinge on what was then my own rather delicate project, a preliminary profile of Treat Morrison for *The New York Times Magazine*, to be followed, if this exploratory drilling went as hoped, by a full-scale study of his proconsular role through six administrations, but it was a little more than that.

I refused such requests because I did not want to be drawn into discussion of whatever elements seemed questionable, whatever details seemed not to be trusted, whatever logical connections seemed to be missing between the Elena Janklow I had known in California (Catherine Janklow's mother, Wynn Janklow's wife, co-chair, committee member, arranger of centerpieces and table favors for a full calendar of benefit lunches and dinners and performances and fashion shows, originator in fact of the locally famous No Ball Ball, enabling the benevolent to send in their checks and stay home) and the Elena McMahon in the two AP stories.

I could find no reasonable excuse not to participate in the subsequent study in crisis management undertaken by the Rand Corporation on behalf of DOD/State, but I was careful: I adopted the vernacular of such studies. I talked about "conflict resolution." I talked about "incident prevention." I did provide facts, more facts even than I was asked to provide, but facts of such stupefying detail and doubtful relevance that none of the several Rand analysts engaged in the project thought to ask the one question I did not want to answer.

The question of course was what did I think had happened.

I thought she got caught in the pipeline, swept into the conduits.

I thought the water was over her head.

I thought she realized what she had been set up to do only in however many elongated seconds there were between the time she registered the presence of the man on the bluff and the time it happened.

I still think this.

I say so now only because real questions have occurred to me.

About the events in question.

At the embassy in question.

At the time in question.

You may recall the rhetoric of the time in question.

This wasn't a situation that lent itself to an MBA analysis.

This wasn't a zero-sum deal.

In a perfect world we might have perfect choices, in the real world we had real choices, and we made them, and we measured the losses against what might have been the gains.

Real world.

There was no doubt certain things happened we might have wished hadn't happened.

There was no doubt we were dealing with forces that might or might not include unpredictable elements.

Elements beyond our control.

No doubt, no argument at all.

And yet.

Still.

Consider the alternatives: trying to create a context for democracy and maybe getting your hands a little dirty in the process or just opting out, letting the other guy call it.

Add it up.

I did that.

I added it up.

Not zero-sum at all.

You could call this a reconstruction. A corrective, if you will, to the Rand study. A revisionist view of a time and a place and an incident about which, ultimately, most people preferred not to know. Real world.

4

If I could believe (as convention tells us) that character is destiny and the past prologue et cetera, I
might begin the story of what happened to Elena
McMahon during the summer of 1984 at some earlier
point. I might begin it in, say, 1964, the year during
which Elena McMahon lost her scholarship to the
University of Nevada and within a week invented herself as a reporter for the Los Angeles *Herald Examiner*. I might begin it four years later, in 1968, the year
during which, in the course of researching a back-
grounder on the development of the oil business
in southern California, Elena McMahon met Wynn
Janklow in his father's office on Wilshire Boulevard
and, with such single-minded efficiency that she never
bothered to write the piece, reinvented herself as
his wife.

Crucible events.

Revelations of character.

Absolutely, no question, but the character they reveal is that of a survivor.

Since what happened to Elena McMahon during the

summer of 1984 had notably little to do with surviving, let me begin where she would begin.

The night she walked off the 1984 campaign.

You will notice that participants in disasters typically locate the "beginning" of the disaster at a point suggesting their own control over events. A plane crash retold will begin not with the pressure system over the Central Pacific that caused the instability over the Gulf that caused the wind shear at DFW but at some manageable human intersect, with for example the "funny feeling" ignored at breakfast. An account of a 6.8 earthquake will begin not at the overlap of the tectonic plates but more comfortably, at the place in London where we ordered the Spode that shattered the morning the tectonic plates shifted.

Had we just gone with the funny feeling. Had we just never ordered the Spode.

We all prefer the magical explanation.

So it was with Elena McMahon.

She had walked off the campaign the day before the California primary at one-forty in the morning Los Angeles time, she repeatedly told the DIA agent Treat Morrison flew down to take her statement, as if the exact time at which she walked off the campaign had set into inexorable motion the sequence of events that followed.

At the time she walked off the campaign she had not seen her father in some months, she told the DIA agent when he pressed her on this point.

How many months exactly, the agent had said.

I don't know exactly, she had said.

Two points. One, Elena McMahon did know exactly how many months it had been since she had last seen her father. Two, the exact number of months between the time Elena McMahon had last seen her father and the time Elena McMahon walked off the campaign was, like the exact time at which she walked off the campaign, not significant. For the record: at the time Elena McMahon walked off the 1984 campaign she had not seen her father in twenty-one months. The last time she had seen him was September 1982, either the fourteenth or the fifteenth. She could date this almost exactly because it had been either the day or the day after Bashir Gemayel was assassinated in Lebanon and at the moment the phone rang she had been sitting at her desk doing White House reaction.

In fact she could date it not almost exactly but exactly.

It had been the fifteenth. September 15 1982.

She knew it had been the fifteenth because she had arrived in Washington on the fifteenth of August and given herself a month to find a house and put Catherine into school and get the raise that meant she was no longer a provisional hire (there again a survivor, there again that single-minded efficiency), and at the moment her father called she had just made a note to ask about the raise.

Hey, her father had said when she picked up the telephone. This was his standard way of initiating telephone contact, no name, no greeting, just *Hey*, then silence. She had outwaited the silence. I'm passing through Washington, he had said then, maybe you could meet me the next half hour or so.

I'm at work, she had said.

Some kind of coincidence, he had said, since that's where I called you.

Because she was on deadline she had told him to meet her across the street at the Madison. This had seemed a convenient neutral venue but as soon as she walked in and saw him sitting alone in the bar, drumming his fingers insistently on the small table, she knew that the Madison had not been a propitious choice. His eyes were narrowed, fixed on three men in apparently identical pin-striped suits at the next table. She recognized one of the three as White House, his name was Christopher Hormel, he was OMB but for whatever reason he had been hovering officiously around the podium during the noon briefing on Lebanon. That's not policy, that's politesse, Christopher Hormel was saying as she sat down, and then he repeated it, as if he had coined a witticism.

Just keep on shoveling it, her father had said.

Christopher Hormel had pushed back his chair and turned.

Spit it out, buddy, what's your problem, her father had said.

Daddy, she had said, an entreaty.

I have no problem, Christopher Hormel had said, and turned away.

Faggots, her father had said, his fingers roaming the little dish of nuts and toasted cereal for the remaining macadamia nut.

Actually you're wrong, she had said.

I see you're buying right into the package here, her father had said. You're very adaptable, anybody ever mention that?

She had ordered him a bourbon and water.

Say Early Times, he had corrected her. You say bourbon in these faggot bars they give you the Sweet

Turkey shit or whatever it's called, then charge extra. And hey, you, pal, crack out the almonds, save the Cheerios for the queers.

When the drink came he had drained it, then hunched forward. He had a small deal going in Alexandria, he had said. He had a source for two or three hundred nines, Intratecs, lame little suckers he could pick up at seventy-five per and pass on for close to three hundred, the guy he passed them to would double his money on the street but let him, that was street, he didn't do street, never had, never would.

Wouldn't need to either.

Because things were hotting up again.

Whole lot of popping going on again.

She had signed the bill.

Hey, Ellie, give us a smile, whole lot of popping.

The next time she saw him was the day she walked off the 1984 campaign.

5

She had not planned to walk off the campaign. She had picked up the plane that morning at Newark and except for the Coke during refueling at Kansas City she had not eaten in twenty-eight hours but she had not once thought of walking away, not on the plane, not at the rally in South Central, not at the meet-and-greet at the Maravilla project, not sitting on the sidewalk in Beverly Hills waiting for the pool report on the celebrity fund-raiser (the celebrity fund-raiser at which most of the guests had turned out to be people she had known in her previous life as Elena Janklow, the celebrity fund-raiser at which in the natural course of her previous life as Elena Janklow she would have been standing under the Regal Rents party tent listening to the candidate and calculating the length of time before she could say good night and drive home to the house on the Pacific Coast Highway and sit on the deck and smoke a cigarette), not even then had she framed the thought *I could walk off this campaign.*

She had performed that day as usual.

She had filed twice.

She had filed first from the Evergreen operations office in Kansas City and she had filed the update during downtime at the Holiday Inn in Torrance. She had received and answered three queries from the desk about why she had elected not to go with a story the wires were moving about an internal poll suggesting shifts among most-likely-voters. *Re your query on last night's Sawyer-Miller poll*, she had typed in response to the most recent query. *For third time, still consider sample too small to be significant.* She had improved the hour spent sitting on the sidewalk waiting for the pool report on the celebrity fund-raiser by roughing in a draft for the Sunday analysis.

She had set aside the seductive familiarity of the celebrity fund-raiser.

The smell of jasmine.

The pool of blue jacaranda petals on the sidewalk where she sat.

The sense that under that tent nothing bad was going to happen and its corollary, the sense that under that tent nothing at all was going to happen.

That had been her old life and this was her new life and it was imperative that she keep focus.

She had kept focus.

She had maintained momentum.

It would seem to her later that nothing about the day had gone remarkably wrong but it would also seem that nothing about the day had gone remarkably right: for example, her name had been left off the manifest at Newark. There was a new Secret Service rotation and she had packed her press tags and the agent in charge had not wanted to let her on the plane. Where's the dog, the agent had said repeatedly to no one in particular. The Port Authority was supposed to have a dog here, where's the dog.

It had been seven in the morning and already hot and they had been standing on the tarmac with the piles of luggage and camera equipment. I talked to Chicago last night, she had said, trying to get the agent to look at her as she groped through her bag trying to find the tags. This was true. She had talked to Chicago the night before and she had also talked to Catherine the night before. Who she had not talked to the night before was her father. Her father had left two messages on her machine in Georgetown but she had not returned the calls. Hey, her father had said the first time he called. Then the breathing, then the click. She located something smooth and hard in her bag and thought she had the tags but it was a tin of aspirin.

We had a real life and now we don't and just because I'm your daughter I'm supposed to like it and I don't, Catherine had said to her.

Pardon my using your time but I've been trying to call your mother and that asshole she lives with refuses to put her on the line, her father had said to her machine the second time he called.

Chicago said I was on the plane, she had said to the agent.

We don't have a dog, it'll take all day to sweep this shit, the agent had said. He seemed to be directing this to a sound tech who squatted on the tarmac rummaging through his equipment.

She had touched the agent's sleeve in an effort to get him to look at her. If somebody would just check with Chicago, she had said.

The agent had retracted his arm abruptly but still had not looked at her.

Who is she, he had said. She hasn't been cleared by the campaign, what's she doing here.

The sound tech had not looked up.

Tell him you know me, she had said to the sound tech. She could not think whose tech he was but she knew that she had seen him on the plane. What she had come during the campaign to describe as her advanced age (since no one ever demurred this had become by June an embarrassing reflex, a tic that made her face flush even as she said it) made asking for help obscurely humiliating but that was not important. What was important was getting on the plane. If she was not on the plane she would not be on the campaign. The campaign had momentum, the campaign had a schedule. The schedule would automatically take her to July, August, the frigid domes with the confetti falling and the balloons floating free.

She would work out the business about Catherine later.

She could handle Catherine.

She would call her father later.

Tell him you know me, she repeated to the sound tech's back.

The sound tech extracted a mult cable from his equipment bag, straightened up and gazed at her, squinting. Then he shrugged and walked away.

I'm always on the plane, I've been on the plane since New Hampshire, she said to the agent, and then amended it: I mean on and off the plane. She could hear the note of pleading in her voice. She remembered: the tech was ABC. During Illinois she had been standing on the edge of a satellite feed and he had knocked her down pushing to get in close.

Tough titty, cunt, I'm working, he had said when she objected.

She watched him bound up the steps, two at a time, and disappear into the DC-9. The bruise where he had pushed her was still discolored two months later. She could feel sweat running down beneath her gabardine jacket and it occurred to her that if he had passed her on the way to the steps she would have tripped him. She had worn the gabardine jacket because California was always cold. If she did not find the tags she would not even get to California. The ABC tech would get to California but she would not. Tough titty, cunt, I'm working. She began to unpack her bag on the tarmac, laying out first tapes and notebooks and then an unopened package of panty hose, evidence of her sincerity, hostages to her insistence that the tags existed.

I just didn't happen to be on the plane this week, she said to the agent. And you just came on. Which is why you don't know me.

The agent adjusted his jacket so that she could see his shoulder holster.

She tried again: I had something personal, so I wasn't on the plane this week, otherwise you would know me.

This too was humiliating.

Why she had not been on the plane this week was none of the agent's business.

I had a family emergency, she heard herself add.

The agent turned away.

Wait, she said. She had located the tags in a pocket of her cosmetics bag and scrambled to catch up with

the agent, leaving her tapes and notebooks and panty
hose exposed on the tarmac as she offered up the
metal chain, the bright oblongs of laminated plastic.
The agent examined the tags and tossed them back to
her, his eyes opaque. By the time she was finally allowed on the plane the camera crews had divided up
the day's box lunches (there was only the roast beef
left from yesterday and the vegetarian, the Knight-
Ridder reporter sitting next to her said, but she hadn't
missed shit because the vegetarian was just yesterday's
roast beef without the roast beef) and the aisle was already slippery from the food fight and somebody had
rigged the PA system to play rap tapes and in the
process disconnected the galley refrigerator. Which
was why, when she walked off the campaign at one-
forty the next morning in the lobby of the Hyatt
Wilshire in Los Angeles, she had not eaten, except for
the Coke during refueling at Kansas City and the gar-
nish of wilted alfalfa sprouts the Knight-Ridder reporter had declined to eat, in twenty-eight hours.

Later she would stress that part.

Later when she called the desk from LAX she
would stress the part about not having eaten in
twenty-eight hours.

She would leave out the part about her father.

*Pardon my using your time but I've been trying to
call your mother and that asshole she lives with refuses to put her on the line.*

She would leave out the part about Catherine.

*We had a real life and now we don't and just
because I'm your daughter I'm supposed to like it and
I don't.*

She would leave out her father and she would leave
out Catherine and she would also leave out the smell

of jasmine and the pool of blue jacaranda petals on the sidewalk outside the celebrity fund-raiser.

Small public company going nowhere, bought it as a tax shelter, knew nothing about the oil business, she had written in her notebook on the day in 1968 when she interviewed Wynn Janklow's father. *I remember I said I wanted to take a look at our oil wells, I remember I stopped at a drugstore to buy film for my camera, little Brownie I had, I'd never seen an oil well before and I wanted to take a picture. And so we drove down to Dominguez Hills there and took a few pictures. At that point in time we were taking out oil sands from twelve to fourteen thousand feet, not enough to reveal viscosity. And today the city of Los Angeles is one of the great oil-producing areas in the world, seventeen producing fields within the city limits. Fox, Hillcrest, Pico near Doheny, Cedars, United Artists, UCLA, five hundred miles of pipeline under the city, the opposition to drilling isn't rational, it's psychiatric, whole time my son was playing ball at Beverly Hills High School there I was taking out oil from a site just off third base, he used to take girls out there, show them my rockers.*

The old man had looked up when the son entered the office.

Just ask him if he didn't, the old man said.

Beverly Hills crude, the son said, and she married him.

Pick yourself up.

Brush yourself off.

I hadn't eaten in twenty-eight hours, she would say to the desk.

Not that it mattered to the desk.

6

On the plane to Miami that morning she had experienced a brief panic, a sense of being stalled, becalmed, like the first few steps off a moving sidewalk. Off the campaign she would get no overnight numbers. Off the campaign she would get no spin, no counterspin, no rumors, no denials. The campaign would be en route to San Jose and her seat on the DC-9 would be empty and she was sitting by herself in this seat she had paid for herself on this Delta flight to Miami. The campaign would move on to Sacramento at noon and San Diego at one and back to Los Angeles at two and she would still be sitting in this seat she had paid for herself on this Delta flight to Miami.

This was just downtime, she told herself. This was just an overdue break. She had been pushing herself too hard, juggling too many balls, so immersed in the story she was blind to the story.

This could even be an alternate way into the story.

In the flush of this soothing interpretation she ordered a vodka and orange juice and fell asleep before it came. When she woke over what must have been Texas she could not at first remember why she was on this sedative but unfamiliar plane. *RON Press Overnites at Hyatt Wilshire,* the Los Angeles schedule had said, and the bus had finally arrived at the Hyatt Wilshire and the press arrangements had been made out of Chicago but her name was not on the list and there was no room.

Chicago fucked up, what else is new, the traveling press secretary had shrugged. So find somebody, double up, wheels up at six sharp.

She recalled a fatigue near vertigo. She recalled standing at the desk for what seemed a long time watching the apparently tireless children with whom she had crossed the country drift toward the bar and the elevator. She recalled picking up her bag and her computer case and walking out into the cold California night in her gabardine jacket and asking the doorman if he could get her a taxi to LAX. She had not called the desk until she had the boarding pass for Miami.

7

When she arrived at the house in Sweetwater at five-thirty that afternoon the screen door was unlatched and the television was on and her father was asleep in a chair, the remote clutched in his hand, a half-finished drink and a can of jalapeño bean dip at his elbow. She had never before seen this house but it was indistinguishable from the house in Hialeah and before that the unit in Opa-Locka and for that matter the place between Houston and NASA. They were just places he rented and they all looked alike. The house in Vegas had looked different. Her mother had still been living with him when they had the house in Vegas.

Pardon my using your time but I've been trying to call your mother and that asshole she lives with refuses to put her on the line.

She would deal with that later.

She had dealt with the plane and she would deal with that.

She sat on a stool at the counter that divided the living room from the kitchen and began reading the Miami *Herald* she had picked up at the airport, very methodically, every page in order, column one to column eight, never turning ahead to the break, only occasionally glancing at the television screen. The Knight-Ridder reporter who had been sitting next to her on the plane the day before appeared to have based his file entirely on the most-likely-voters story the wires had moved. *California political insiders are predicting a dramatic last-minute shift in primary voting patterns here,* his story began, misleadingly. An American hostage who had walked out of Lebanon via Damascus said at his press conference in Wiesbaden that during captivity he had lost faith not only in the teachings of his church but in God. *Hostage Describes Test of Faith,* the headline read, again misleadingly. She considered ways in which the headline could have been made accurate (*Hostage Describes Loss of Faith? Hostage Fails Test of Faith?*), then put down the *Herald* and studied her father. He had gotten old. She had called him at Christmas and she had talked to him from Laguna last week but she had not seen him and at some point in between he had gotten old.

She was going to have to tell him again about her mother.

Pardon my using your time but I've been trying to call your mother and that asshole she lives with refuses to put her on the line.

She had told him on the telephone from Laguna but it had not gotten through, she was going to have to tell him again, he would want to talk about it.

It occurred to her suddenly that this was why she was here.

She had arrived at LAX with every intention of returning to Washington and had heard herself asking instead for a flight to Miami.

She had asked for a flight to Miami because she was going to have to tell him again about her mother.

That her mother had died was not going to change the course of his days but it would be a subject, it was something they would need to get through.

They would not need to talk about Catherine. Or rather: he would ask how Catherine was and she would say fine and then he would ask if Catherine liked school and she would say yes.

She should call Catherine. She should let Catherine know where she was.

We had a real life and now we don't and just because I'm your daughter I'm supposed to like it and I don't.

She would call Catherine later. She would call Catherine the next day.

Her father snored, a ragged apnea snore, and the remote dropped from his hand. On the television screen the graphic *Broward Closeup* appeared, over film of what seemed to be a mosque in Pompano Beach. It developed that discussion of politics had been forbidden at this mosque because many of what the reporter called Pompano Muslims came from countries at war with one another. "In Broward County at least," the reporter concluded, "Muslims who have known only war can now find peace."

This too was misleading. It occurred to her that possibly what was misleading was the concept of "news" itself, a liberating thought. She picked up the remote and pressed the mute.

"Goddamn ragheads," her father said, but did not open his eyes.

"Daddy," she said tentatively.

"Goddamn ragheads deserve to get nuked." He opened his eyes. "Kitty. Don't. Jesus Christ. Don't do that."

"It's not Kitty," she said. "It's her daughter. Your daughter."

She did not know how long she had been crying but when she groped in her bag for a tissue she found only damp wads.

"It's Elena," she said finally. "It's me."

"Ellie," her father said. "What the hell."

That would be one place to begin this story.

Elena McMahon's father getting involved with the people who wanted to make the deal with Fidel to take back the Sans Souci would have been another.

Way back. Much earlier. Call that back story.

This would have been another place to begin, also back story, just an image: a single-engine Cessna flying low, dropping a roll of toilet paper over a mangrove clearing, the paper streaming and looping as it catches on the treetops, the Cessna gaining altitude as it banks to retrace its flight path. A man, Elena McMahon's father, the man in the house in Sweetwater but much younger, retrieves the cardboard roll, its ends closed with masking tape. He cuts the masking tape with an army knife. He takes out a piece of paper. *Suspend all activity*, the paper reads. *Report without delay*.

November 22 1963.

Dick McMahon's footnote to history.

Treat Morrison was in Indonesia the day that roll of toilet paper drifted down over the Keys.

On special assignment at the consulate in Surabaya. They locked the consulate doors and did not open them for three days.

Treat Morrison's own footnote to history.

8

I still believe in history.

Let me amend that.

I still believe in history to the extent that I believe history to be made exclusively and at random by people like Dick McMahon. There are still more people like Dick McMahon around than you might think, most of them old but still doing a little business, keeping a hand in, an oar in the water, the wolf from the door. They can still line up some jeeps in Shreveport, they can still lay hands on some slots in Beaumont, they can still handle the midnight call from the fellow who needs a couple or three hundred Savage automatic rifles with telescopic sights. They may not remember all the names they used but they remember the names they did not use. They may have trouble sorting out the details of all they knew but they remember having known it.

They remember they ran some moves.

They remember they had personal knowledge of certain actions.

They remember they knew Carlos Prío, they remember they heard certain theories about his suicide. They remember they knew Johnny Roselli, they remember they heard certain theories about how he turned up in the oil drum in Biscayne Bay. They remember many situations in which certain fellows show up in the middle of the night asking for something and a couple or three days later these same identical fellows turn up in San Pedro Sula or Santo Domingo or Panama right in the goddamn thick of it.

Christ if I had a dollar for every time somebody came to me and said he was thinking about doing a move I'd be a rich man today, Elena McMahon's father said the day she was going down to where he berthed the *Kitty Rex*.

For the first two weeks at the house in Sweetwater she conserved energy by not noticing anything. That was how she put it to herself, she was conserving energy, as if attention were a fossil fuel. She drove out to Key Biscayne and let her mind go fallow, absorbing only the bleached flatness of the place, the pale aquamarine water and the gray sky and the drifts of white coral sand and the skeletons of live oak and oleander broken when the storms rolled in. One day when it rained and the wind was blowing she walked across the lowest of the causeways, overcome by a need to feel the water lapping over her sandals. By then she had already shed her clothes, pared down to essentials, concentrated her needs, wrapped up her gabardine jacket and unopened packages of panty hose and dropped them, a tacit farewell to the distractions of the temperate zone, in a Goodwill box on Eighth Street.

There's some question here what you're doing, the desk had said when she called to say she was in Miami. Siegel's been covering for you, but you understand we'll need to move someone onto this on a through-November basis.

That would be fair, she had said.

She had not yet conserved enough energy to resume thinking on a through-November basis.

At a point late each day she would focus on finding something that her father would eat, something he would not immediately set aside in favor of another drink, and she would go downtown to a place she remembered he liked and ask for containers of black beans or shrimp in garlic sauce she could reheat later.

From the Floridita, she would say when her father looked without interest at his plate.

In Havana, he would say, doubtful.

The one here, she would say. The Floridita on Flagler Street. You used to take me there.

The Floridita your mother and I knew was in Havana, he would say.

Which would lead as if on replay to his telling her again about the night at the Floridita in he believed 1958 with her mother and Carlos Prío and Fidel and one of the Murchisons. The Floridita in Havana, he would specify each time. Havana was the Floridita your mother and I knew, goddamn but we had some fun there, just ask your mother, she'll tell you.

Which would lead in the same replay mode to her telling him again that her mother was dead. On each retelling he would seem to take it in. Goddamn, he would say. Kitty's gone. He would make her repeat certain details, as if to fix the flickering fact of it.

She had not known how sick Kitty was, no.

She had not seen Kitty before she died, no.

There had been no funeral, no.

Kitty had been cremated, yes.

Kitty's last husband was named Ward, yes.

It was true that Ward used to sell pharmaceuticals, yes, but no, she would not describe it as dealing dope and no, she did not think there had been any funny business. In any case Ward was beside the point, which was this: her mother was dead.

Her father's eyes would go red then, and he would turn away.

Pretty Kitty, he would say as if to himself. Kit-Cat.

Half an hour later he would again complain that he had tried to call Kitty a night or two before and the asshole dope dealer she lived with had refused to put her on the line.

Because he couldn't, Elena would say again. Because she's dead.

Sometimes when the telephone rang in the middle of the night she would wake, and hear the front door close and a car engine turning over, her father's '72 Cadillac Seville convertible, parked on the spiky grass outside the room in which she slept. The head-lights would sweep the ceiling of the room as he backed out onto the street. Most nights she would get up and open a bottle of beer and sit in bed drinking it until she fell asleep again, but one night the beer did not work and she was still awake, standing barefoot in the kitchen watching a local telethon on which a West Palm Beach resident in a sequined dress seemed to be singing gospel, when her father came in at dawn.

What the hell, her father said.

I said to Satan get thee behind me, the woman in the sequined dress was singing on the television screen.

You shouldn't be driving, Elena said.

Victory today is mine.

Right, I should take out my teeth and go to the nursing home, he said. Jesus Christ, you want to kill me too?

The woman in the sequined dress snapped her mike cord as she segued into "After You've Been There Ten Thousand Years," and Dick McMahon transferred his flickering rage to the television screen. I been there ten thousand years I still won't want to see you, honey, he shouted at the woman in the sequined dress. Because honey you are worthless, you are worse than worthless, you are trash. By the time he refocused on Elena he had softened, or forgotten. How about a drink, he said.

She got him a drink.

If you have any interest in what I'm doing, he said as she sat down at the table across from him, all I can say is it's major.

She said nothing. She had trained herself since childhood not to have any interest in what her father was doing. This had been difficult only when she had to fill out a form that asked for *Father's Occupation*. He did deals. *Does deals?* No. She had usually settled on *Investor*. If it came up in conversation she would say that her father bought and sold things, leaving open the possibility, in those parts of the country where she had lived until 1982, raw sunbelt cities riding high on land trades, that what he bought and sold was real estate. She had lost her scholarship at the University of Nevada because the administration had changed the basis for granting aid from merit to need and she had recognized that it would be a waste of time to ask her father to fill out a financial report.

Right from the top, he said. Top shelf.

She said nothing.

37

This one turns out the way it's supposed to turn out, he said, I'll be in a position to deal myself out, fold my hand, take the *Kitty Rex* down past Largo and stay there. Some life. Catching fish and bumming around the shallows. Not my original idea of a good time but it beats sitting here getting old.

Who exactly is running this one, she said carefully.

What do you care, he said, suddenly wary. What did you ever care who was running any of them.

I mean, she said, how did whoever is running this one happen to decide to work through you.

Why wouldn't they work through me, he said. I still got my teeth. I'm not in the nursing home yet. No thanks to you.

Dick McMahon had closed his eyes, truculent, and had not woken until she took the glass from his hand and put a cotton blanket over his legs.

What do you hear from your mother, he had said then.

9

That was the morning, June 15, a Friday, when she should have known it was time to cut and run.

She knew how to cut and run.

She had done it often enough.

Cut and run, cut her losses, just walked away.

She had just walked away from her mother for example.

See where it got her.

She had flown to Laguna as soon as she got the call but there had been no funeral. Her connection into John Wayne was delayed and by the time she arrived in the cold May twilight her mother had already been cremated. You know how Kitty felt about funerals, Ward said repeatedly. Actually I never heard her mention funerals, Elena said finally, thinking only to hear more about what her mother had said or thought, but Ward had looked at her as if wounded. She was welcome, he said, to do what she wanted with the cremains, the remains, the ashes or whatever, the cremains was what they called them, but in case she had nothing specific in mind he had already arranged with the Neptune Society. You know how Kitty felt about open ocean, he said. Open ocean was something else Elena did not recall her mother mentioning. So if it's all the same to you, Ward said, visibly relieved by her silence, I'll go ahead with the arrangements as planned.

She found herself wondering how short a time she could reasonably stay.

There would be nothing out of John Wayne but she could get a redeye out of LAX.

Straight shot up the 405.

Ward's daughter Belinda was in the bedroom, packing what she called the belongings. The belongings would go to the hospice thrift shop, Belinda said, but she knew that Kitty would want Elena to take what she wanted. Elena opened a drawer, aware of Belinda watching her.

Kitty never got tired of mentioning you, Belinda said. I'd be over here dealing with the Medicare forms or some other little detail and she'd find a way to mention you. It might be you'd just called from wherever.

The drawer seemed to be filled with turbans, snoods, shapeless head coverings of a kind Elena could not associate with her mother.

Or, Belinda said, it might be that you hadn't. I got her those for the chemo.

Elena closed the drawer.

Moved by the dim wish to preserve something of her mother from consignment to the hospice thrift shop she tried to remember objects in which her mother had set special stock, but in the end took only an ivory bracelet she remembered her mother wearing and a creased snapshot, retrieved from a carton grease-penciled OUT, of her mother and father seated in folding metal lawn chairs on either side of a portable barbecue outside the house in Las Vegas. Before she left she stood in the kitchen watching Ward demonstrate his ability to microwave one of the several dozen individual casseroles stacked in the freezer. Your mother did those just before she went down, Belinda said, raising her voice over *Jeopardy*. Kitty would have aced that, Ward said when a contestant on-screen missed a question in the Famous Travelers category. See what he does, Belinda said as if Ward could not hear. He keeps working in Kitty's name, same way Kitty used to work in yours. Two hours later Elena had been at LAX, trying to get cash from an ATM and unable to remember either her bank code or her mother's maiden name.

It might be you'd just called from wherever.

In the deep nowhere safety of the United lounge she drank two glasses of water and tried to remember her calling card number.

Or it might be that you hadn't.

Thirty-six hours after that she had been on the tarmac at Newark with the agent saying where's the dog, we don't have a dog, it'll take all day to sweep this shit.

She had cut and run from that too.

No more schedules, no more confetti, no more balloons floating free.

She had walked away from that the way she had walked away from the house on the Pacific Coast Highway. She did not think Wynn, she thought the house on the Pacific Coast Highway.

Tile floors, white walls, tennis lunches on Sunday afternoons.

Men with even tans and recent manicures, women

with killer serves and bodies minutely tuned against stretch marks; always an actor or two or three, often a player just off the circuit. *The beauty part is, the Justice Department still gets its same take,* Wynn would be saying on the telephone, and then, his hand over the receiver, *Tell whoever you got in the kitchen it's time to lay on the lunch.* Nothing about those Sunday afternoons would have changed except this: Wynn's office, not Elena, would now call the caterer who laid on the lunch.

The big Stellas would still flank the door.

Wynn would still wake at night when the tide reached ebb and the sea went silent.

Goddamn what's the matter out there.

Smell of jasmine, pool of jacaranda, blue so intense you could drown in it.

We had a real life and now we don't and just because I'm your daughter I'm supposed to like it and I don't.

What exactly did you have in Malibu you don't have now, she had asked Catherine, and Catherine had walked right into it, Catherine had never even seen it coming. You could open the door in Malibu and be at the beach, Catherine said. Or the Jacuzzi. Or the pool.

Anything else, she had asked Catherine, her voice neutral.

The tennis court.

Is that all.

The three cars, Catherine said after a silence. We had three cars.

A Jacuzzi, she had said to Catherine. A pool. A tennis court. Three cars. Is that your idea of a real life?

Catherine, humiliated, outmaneuvered, had slammed down the phone.

Smell of jasmine, pool of jacaranda.

An equally indefensible idea of a real life.

She had been thinking that over when Catherine called back.

I had my father thank you very much.

She was even about to just walk away from Catherine.

She knew she was. She knew the signs. She was losing focus on Catherine. She was losing momentum on Catherine. If she could even consider walking away from Catherine she could certainly walk away from this house in Sweetwater. That she did not was the beginning of the story as some people in Miami came to see it.

10

"I have frequently stated that I did not intend to set down either autobiographical notes of any kind or any version of events as I have witnessed and affected them. It has been my firm and long-held conviction that events, for better or for worse, speak for themselves, work as it were toward their own ends. After reviewing published accounts of certain of these events, however, I find my own role in them to have been misrepresented. Therefore, on this August Sunday morning, with a tropical storm due from the southeast and hard rain already falling outside these offices I am about to vacate at the Department of State in the City of Washington, District of Columbia, I have determined to set forth as concisely as possible, and in as much detail as is consistent with national security, certain actions I took in 1984 in the matter of what later became known as the lethal, as opposed to the humanitarian, resupply."

So begins the four-hundred-and-seventy-six-page transcript of the taped statement that Treat Morrison committed to the Bancroft Library at Berkeley with instructions that it be sealed to scholars until five years after his death.

Those five years have now passed.

As have, and this would have been his calculation, any lingering spasms of interest in the matter of what later became known as the lethal, as opposed to the humanitarian, resupply.

Or so it would seem.

Since, seven years after Treat Morrison's death and two years after the unsealing of the transcript, I remain the single person to have asked to see it.

MORRISON, TREAT AUSTIN, ambassador-at-large; b. San Francisco Mar. 3, 1930; s. Francis J. and Margaret (Austin) M; B.A., U. of Calif. at Berkeley, 1951; grad. National War College 1956; m. Diane Waring, Dec. 5, 1953 (dec. 1983). Commissioned 2nd lt. U.S. Army 1951, served in Korea, Germany, mil. attaché Chile 1953-54; spec. asst to commander SHAPE Paris 1955; attaché to US Mission to E.C. Brussels 1956-57

So Treat Morrison's *Who's Who* entry began.

And continued.

All the special postings enumerated, all the private-sector sojourns specified.

All there.

Right down to *Office: Dept. of State, 2201 C St., N.W., Washington, D.C. 20520.*

Without giving the slightest sense of what Treat Morrison actually did.

Which was fix things.

45

What was remarkable about those four hundred and seventy-six pages that Treat Morrison committed to the Bancroft Library was, as in his *Who's Who* entry, less what was said than what was not said. What was said was predictable enough, *globalism versus regionalism, full Boland, failed nations, correct interventions, multilateral approach, Directive 25, Resolution 427, criteria not followed*, nothing Treat Morrison could not have said at the Council on Foreign Relations, nothing he had not said, up there in the paneled room with the portrait of David Rockefeller and the old guys nodding off and the young guys asking pinched textbook questions and the willowy young women who worked on the staff standing in the back of the room like geishas, shuttle up and hop a flight back down with one of the corporate guys, maybe learn something for a change, you'd be surprised, they've got their own projections, their own risk analysts, no bureaucracy, no commitments to stale ideologies, none of those pinched textbook questions, they can afford to keep out there ahead of the power curve, corporate guys are light-years ahead of us.

Sometimes.

Four hundred and seventy-six pages on correct interventions and no clue that a correct intervention was for Treat Morrison an intervention in which when you run out of options you can still get your people to the airport.

Four hundred and seventy-six pages with only a veiled suggestion of Treat Morrison's rather spectacular indifference to the conventional interests and concerns of his profession, only an oblique flash of his particular maladaption, which was to be a manipulator of abstracts whose exclusive interest was in the specific. You get just the slightest hint of that maladaption in *tropical storm due from the southeast and hard rain already falling*, just the barest lapse before the sonorous recovery of *outside these offices I am about to vacate at the Department of State in the City of Washington, District of Columbia.*

No hint at all of his long half-mad gaze.

Wide spindrift gaze toward paradise, Elena Mc-Mahon said the first time she was alone with him.

He said nothing.

A poem, she said.

Still he said nothing.

Something *galleons of Carib fire*, she said, something something *the seal's wide spindrift gaze toward paradise.*

He studied her without speaking. Diane read poetry, he said then.

There had been a silence.

Diane was his wife.

Diane was dead.

Diane Morrison, 52, wife of, after a short illness, survived by, in lieu of flowers.

I wasn't thinking about the Carib fire part, Elena had said finally.

Yes you were, Treat Morrison had said.

I I

What we want here is a montage, music over. *Angle on Elena*. Alone on the dock where her father berthed the *Kitty Rex*. Working loose a splinter on the planking with the toe of her sandal. Taking off her scarf and shaking out her hair, damp from the sweet heavy air of South Florida. *Cut to Barry Sedlow*. Standing in the door of the frame shack, under the sign that read RENTALS GAS BAIT BEER AMMO. Leaning against the counter. Watching Elena through the screen door as he waited for change. *Angle on the manager*. Sliding a thousand-dollar bill beneath the tray in the cash register, replacing the tray, counting out the hundreds.

No place you could not pass a hundred.

There in the sweet heavy air of South Florida.

Havana so close you could see the two-tone Impalas on the Malecón.

Goddamn but we had some fun there.

The music would give you the sweet heavy air, the music would give you Havana.

Imagine what the music was as: Barry Sedlow folded the bills into his money clip without looking at them, kicked open the screen door, and walked down the dock, a little something in the walk, a definite projection of what a woman less wary than Elena might (*might, could, would, did, wanted to, needed to*) mistake for sex.

Close on Elena. Watching Barry Sedlow.

"Looks like you're waiting for somebody," Barry Sedlow said.

"I think you," Elena McMahon said.

Her father had begun to run the fever during the evening of Saturday the sixteenth of June. She had known something was wrong because the drink he had made at seven remained untouched at ten, its color mottled by melted ice.

"I don't know what that foul ball expected to get out of showing up here," he said about midnight.

"What foul ball," she said.

"What's his name, Epperson, Max Epperson, the guy you were cozying up with tonight."

She said nothing.

"Come on," he said. "Cat got your tongue?"

"I don't remember seeing anyone but you tonight," she said finally.

"Epperson. Not the guy with the mickey-mouse vest. The other one."

She had framed her response carefully. "I guess neither of them made an impression on me."

"Epperson made an impression on you all right."

She had thought this over. "Listen to me," she had said then. "No one was here."

"Have it your way," he said.

She had driven to an all-night drugstore to buy a

thermometer. His temperature, when she managed to take it, was 102. By morning it was 103.2, and she took him to the emergency room at Jackson Memorial. It was not the nearest hospital but it was the one she knew, a director she and Wynn knew had been shooting there, Catherine had been on spring vacation and they had taken her to visit the location. Nothing straight bourbon won't fix, her father said in the emergency room when the triage nurse asked what was wrong with him. By noon he had been admitted and she had signed the forms and heard the difference between Medicare A and B and when she got back upstairs to the room he had already tried to yank out the IV line and there was blood all over the sheets and he was crying.

"Get me out of here," he said. "Goddamnit get me out of here."

The IV nurse was on another floor and by the time she got back and got the line running again the nurse with the narcotics keys was on another floor and it was close to five before they got him sedated. By dawn his temperature had dropped below 101 but he was focused exclusively on Max Epperson. Epperson was welshing on his word. Epperson had floated a figure of three dollars per for 69s and now he was claiming the market had dropped to two per. Somebody had to talk reason to Epperson, Epperson could queer the whole deal, Epperson was off the reservation, didn't know the first thing about the business he was in.

"I'm not sure I know what business Epperson is in," she said.

"Christ, what business are they all in," her father said.

They would need more blood work before they had

a diagnosis, the resident said. The resident was wearing a pink polo shirt and kept his eyes fixed on the nurses' station, as if to distance himself from the situation and from Elena. They would need a scan, an MRI, they would need something else she did not get the name of. They would of course order a psychiatric evaluation, although evidence of mental confusion would not in itself be a diagnostic criterion. Such mental confusion, if there was mental confusion, was incidental, a secondary complication. Whatever the diagnosis, it would not be uncommon to see a psychotic break with a fever this high in a patient this age.

"He's not that old," she said. This was pointlessly argumentive but she disliked the resident. "He's seventy-four."

"After retirement you have to expect a deficit."

"He's not retired either." She could not seem to stop herself. "He's quite active."

The resident shrugged.

At noon a second resident arrived to do the psychiatric evaluation. He too was wearing a polo shirt, mint green, and he too avoided Elena's eyes. She had fixed her gaze on the signs posted in the room and tried not to listen. I/O. INFECTIOUS SHARPS ONLY. "This is just a little game," the psychiatric resident said. "Can you tell me the name of the current president of the United States."

"Some game," Dick McMahon said.

"Take your time," the psychiatric resident said. "Don't let me rush you."

"Count on it."

There was a silence.

"Daddy," Elena said.

"I get the game," Dick McMahon said. "I'm supposed to say Herbert Hoover, then he puts me away in the home." His eyes narrowed. "All right. *Wheel of Fortune*. Herbert Hoover." He paused, watching the psychiatric resident. "Franklin Delano Roosevelt. Harry S Truman. Dwight David Eisenhower. John Fitzgerald Kennedy. Lyndon Baines Johnson. Richard Milhous Nixon. Gerald whatever his name was, kept tripping over his feet. Jimmy something. The Christer. Then the one now. The one the old dummy's not meant to remember. The other old dummy. Reagan."

"Really excellent, Mr. McMahon," the psychiatric resident said. "You deserve first prize."

"First prize is, you leave." Dick McMahon turned with difficulty away from the resident and closed his eyes. When he opened them again he focused on Elena. "Funny coincidence, that asshole bringing up presidents, which brings us back to Epperson." His voice was exhausted, matter-of-fact. "Because Epperson was involved in Dallas, that deal. I ever tell you that?"

Elena looked at him. His gaze was trusting, his pale-blue eyes rimmed with red. It had not before occurred to her that he might have known who was involved in Dallas. Neither did it surprise her. She supposed if she thought about it that he might have known who was involved in a lot of things, but it was too late now, the processor was unreliable. An exploration of what Dick McMahon knew could now yield only corrupted files, crossed data, lost clusters in which the spectral Max Epperson would materialize not only at the Texas Book Depository but in a room at the Lorraine Hotel in Memphis with Sirhan Sirhan and Santos Trafficante and Fidel and one of the Murchisons.

"What deal in Dallas is that, Mr. McMahon," the psychiatric resident said.

"Just a cattle deal he did in Texas." Elena guided the resident to the door. "He should sleep now. He's too tired for this."

"Don't tell me he's still here," Dick McMahon said without opening his eyes.

"He just left." Elena sat in the chair by the hospital bed and took her father's hand. "It's all right. Nobody's here."

Several times during the next few hours her father woke and asked what time it was, what day it was, each time with an edge of panic in his voice.

He had to be somewhere.

He had some things to do, some people to see.

Some people would be waiting for him to call.

These things he had to do could not wait.

These people he had to see had to be seen now.

Late in the day the sky went dark and she opened the window to feel the air beginning to move. It was only then, while the lightning forking on the horizon and the sound of thunder created a screen, a safe zone in which things could be said that would have no consequences, that Dick McMahon began to tell Elena who it was he had to see, what it was he had to do. *Tropical storm due from the southeast and hard rain already falling.* That he could not do it was obvious. That she should undertake to do it for him would have been less obvious.

12

It is hard now to call up the particular luridity of 1984. I read back over the clips and want only to give you the period verbatim, the fever of it, the counterfeit machismo of it, the extent to which it was about striking and maintaining a certain kind of sentimental pose. Many people appear to have walked around the dead center of this period with parrots on their shoulders, or monkeys. Many people appear to have chosen during this period to identify themselves as something other than what they were, as "cargo specialists" or as "aircraft brokers" or as "rose importers" or, with what came to seem baffling frequency, as "Danish journalists." This was a period during which many people appear to have known that the way to fly undetected over the Gulf coastline of the United States was low and slow, five hundred to a thousand feet, an effortless fade into the helicopter traffic off the Gulf rigs. This was a period during which many people appear to have known that the way to fly undetected over foreign coastlines was with cash, to buy a window. This was a period during which a significant minority among the population at large appears to have understood how government funds earmarked for humanitarian aid might be diverted, even as the General Accounting Office monitored the accounts, to more pressing needs.

Piece of cake, Barry Sedlow told Elena McMahon.

This was not his personal line of work but he knew guys who did it.

Pick a small retailer in any friendly, say Honduras or Costa Rica. Ask this retailer for an invoice showing a written estimate for the purchase of, say, a thousand pairs of green Lee jeans, a thousand green T-shirts, and a thousand pairs of green rubber boots. Specify that the word "estimate" not appear on the invoice. Present this invoice, bearing an estimated figure of say $25,870 but no indication that it is merely an estimate, to the agency responsible for disbursing said humanitarian aid, and ask that the $25,870 reimbursement due be transferred to your account at Citibank Panama. Instruct Citibank Panama to wire the $25,870 to one or another "broker" account, for example the account of a third-party company at the Consolidated Bank in Miami, an account the sole purpose of which is to receive the funds and make them available for whatever need presents itself.

The need, say, to make a payment to Dick McMahon.

There are people who understand this kind of transaction and there are people who do not. Those who understand it are at heart storytellers, weavers of conspiracy just to make the day come alive, and they see it in a flash, comprehend all its turns, get its possibilities. For anyone who could look at a storefront in Honduras or Costa Rica and see an opportunity to tap into the United States Treasury for $25,870, this was a period during which no information could be without interest. Every moment could be seen to connect to every other moment, every act to have logical if obscure consequences, an unbroken narrative of vivid complexity. That Elena McMahon walked into this heightened life and for a brief period lived it is what interests me about her, because she was not one of those who saw in a flash how every moment could connect.

I had thought to learn Treat Morrison's version of why she did it from the transcript of his taped statement. I had imagined that she would have told him what she would not or did not tell either the FBI or the DIA agents who spoke to her. I had imagined that Treat Morrison would have in due time set down his conclusions about whatever it was she told him.

No hint of that in those four hundred and seventy-six pages.

Instead I learned that what he referred to as "a certain incident that occurred in 1984 in connection with one of our Caribbean embassies" should not, in his opinion, have occurred.

Should not have occurred and could not have been predicted.

By what he called "any quantitative measurement."

However, he added. One caveat. *In situ* this certain incident could have been predicted.

Which went to the question, he said, of whether policy should be based on what was said or believed or wished for by people sitting in climate-controlled rooms in Washington or New York or whether policy should be based on what was seen and reported by the people who were actually on the ground. He was constrained by classification from discussing the details of this incident and mentioned it only, he said, as a relevant illustration of the desirability of listening to the people who were actually on the ground.

No comment, as the people who were actually on the ground were trained to say if asked what they were doing or where they were staying or if they wanted a drink or even what time it was.

No comment.

Thank you.

Goodbye.

Elena McMahon had not been trained to say this, but was on the ground nonetheless.

I recently sat at dinner in Washington next to a reporter who covered the ground in question during the period in question. After a few glasses of wine he turned to me, lowered his voice, and said about this experience that nothing that had happened to him since, including the birth of his children and assignment to several more overt wars in several more overt parts of the world, had made him feel so alive as waking up on that particular ground any day in that particular period.

Until Elena McMahon woke up on that particular ground, she did not count her life as one in which anything had happened.

No comment. Thank you. Goodbye.

13

The first time she met Barry Sedlow was the day her father left the hospital. You'll be pleased to know you'll be leaving here tomorrow, the resident had said to her father, and she had followed him out to the nurses' station. "He's not ready to go home," she had said to the resident's back.

"Not to go home, no." The resident had not looked up from the chart he was studying. "Which is why you should be making whatever arrangements you prefer with the discharge coordinator."

"But you just agreed with me. He's not ready to be discharged. The arrangement I prefer is that he stay in the hospital."

"He can't stay in the hospital," the resident said, implacable. "So he will be discharged. And he's not going to be able to take care of himself."

"Exactly. That was my point." She tried for a reasonable tone. "As you say, he's not going to be able to take care of himself. Which is why I think he should stay in the hospital."

"You have the option of making an acceptable arrangement for home care with the discharge coordinator."

"Acceptable to who?"

"To the discharge coordinator."

"So it's up to the discharge coordinator whether or not he stays here?"

"No, it's up to Dr. Mertz."

"I've never met Dr. Mertz."

"Dr. Mertz is the admitting physician of record. On my recommendation, Dr. Mertz has authorized discharge."

"Then I should talk to Dr. Mertz?"

"Dr. Mertz is not on call this week."

She had tried another tack. "Look. If this has something to do with insurance, I signed papers saying I would be responsible. I'll pay for whatever his insurance won't cover."

"You will, yes. But he still won't stay here."

"Why won't he?"

"Because unless you've made an acceptable alternate arrangement," the resident said, unscrewing the top from his fountain pen and wiping the nib with a tissue, "he'll be discharged in the morning to a convalescent facility."

"You can't do that. I won't take him there."

"You won't have to. The facility sends its van."

"I didn't mean that. I meant you can't just send someone to a nursing home."

"Yes. We can. We do it all the time. Unless of course the family has made an acceptable alternate arrangement with the discharge coordinator."

There had been a silence. "How do I reach the discharge coordinator," she said then.

"I could ask her to come by the patient's room." The resident had refitted the top of his pen and placed it in the breast pocket of his polo shirt. He seemed not to know what to do with the tissue. "When she has a moment."

"Somebody took my goddamn shoes," her father had said when she walked back into the room. He was sitting on the edge of the bed buckling his belt and trying to free his arm from the hospital gown. "I can't get out of here without my goddamn shoes." She had no way of knowing whether he intended to walk out or had merely misunderstood the resident, but she had found his shoes and his shirt and arranged his jacket over his thin shoulders, then walked him out past the nurses' station into the elevator.

"You'll need a nurse," she had said tentatively when the elevator doors closed.

Her father had nodded, apparently resigned to strategic compromise.

"I'll tell the agency we need someone right away," she had said, trying to consolidate her gain. "Today."

Once more her father had nodded.

Lulled by the ease of the end run around the hospital apparat, Elena was still basking in this new tractability when, a few hours later, securely back at the house in Sweetwater, the nurse installed in front of the television set and the bed freshly made and a glass of bourbon-spiked Ensure at the ready (another strategic compromise, this one with the nurse), Dick McMahon announced that he needed his car keys and he needed them now.

"I told you," he said when she asked why. "I've got somebody to see. Somebody's waiting for me."

"I told you," he said when she asked who. "I told you the whole deal."

"You have to listen to me," she had said finally. "You're not in any condition to do anything. You're weak. You're still not thinking clearly. You'll make a mistake. You'll get hurt."

Her father had at first said nothing, his pale eyes watery and fixed on hers.

"You don't know what's going to happen," he said then. His voice was helpless, bewildered. "Goddamn, what's going to happen now."

"I just don't want you to get hurt."

"Jesus Christ," he said then, as if defeated, his head falling to one side. "I needed this deal."

She had taken his hand.

"What's going to happen now," he had repeated.

"I'll take care of it," she had said.

Which was how Elena McMahon happened, an hour later, to be standing on the dock where the *Kitty Rex* was berthed. *Looks like you're waiting for somebody*, Barry Sedlow said. *I think you*, Elena McMahon said.

The second time she was to meet Barry Sedlow he had instructed her to be in the lobby of the Omni Hotel on Biscayne Boulevard at what he called thirteen sharp. She was to sit near the entrance to the restaurant as if she were waiting to meet someone for lunch.

There would be lunch traffic in and out of the restaurant, she would not stand out.

If he happened not to show up by the time the lunch traffic thinned out she was to leave, because at that point she would stand out.

"Why might you happen not to show up," she had asked.

Barry Sedlow had written an 800 number on the back of a card reading KROME GUN CLUB and given it to her before he answered. "Could happen I won't like the look of it," he had said then.

She had arrived at one. It had been raining hard all morning and there was water everywhere, water sluicing down the black tile wall behind the lobby pool, water roiling and bubbling over the underwater spots in the pool, water standing on flat roofs and puddling around vents and driving against the six-story canted window. In the chill of the air-conditioning her clothes were damp and clammy against her skin and after a while she stood up and walked around the lobby, trying to get warm. Even the music from the merry-go-round in the mall downstairs was muted, distorted, as if she were hearing it underwater. She was standing at the railing looking down at the merry-go-round when the woman spoke to her.

The woman was holding an unfolded map.

The woman did not want to bother Elena but wondered if she knew the best way to get on I-95.

Elena told her the best way to get on I-95.

At three o'clock the restaurant had emptied out and Barry Sedlow had not appeared. From a pay phone in the lobby she dialed the 800 number Barry Sedlow had given her and found that it was a beeper. She punched in the number of the pay phone in the Omni lobby but at four o'clock, when the phone had not rung, she left.

At midnight the phone rang in the house in Sweetwater.

Elena hesitated, then picked it up.

"You stood out," Barry Sedlow said. "You let yourself be noticed."

"Noticed by who?"

He did not respond directly. "Here's what you're going to want to do."

What she was going to want to do, he said, was walk into the Pan Am Clipper Club at the Miami airport the next day at noon sharp. What she was going to want to do was go to the desk and ask for Michelle. She was going to want to tell Michelle that she was meeting Gary Barnett.

"Who exactly is Gary Barnett," she said.

"Michelle's the blonde, not the spic. Make sure it's Michelle you talk to. The spic is Adele, Adele doesn't know me."

"Gary Barnett is you?"

"Just do it my way for a change."

She had done it his way.

Gary wants you to make yourself comfortable, Michelle had said.

If I could please see your Clipper Club card, Adele had said.

Michelle had rolled her eyes. I *saw* her *card*, Michelle had said.

Elena sat down. On a corner sofa a portly man in a silk suit was talking on the telephone, his voice rising and falling, an unbroken flow of English and Spanish, now imploring, now threatening, oblivious to the announcements of flights for Guayaquil and Panama and Guatemala, oblivious to Elena, oblivious even to the woman at his side, who was thin and gray-haired and wore a cashmere cardigan and expensive walking shoes.

Mr. Lee, the man kept saying.

Then, finally: Let me ask you one question, Mr. Lee. Do we have the sugar or don't we. All right then. You tell me we have it. Then explain to me this one thing. How do we prove we have it. Because believe me, Mr. Lee, we are losing credibility with the buyer. All right. Listen. Here is the situation. We have ninety-two million dollars tied up since Thursday. This is Tuesday. Believe me, ninety-two million dollars is not small change. Is not chicken shit, Mr. Lee. The telex was supposed to be sent on Friday. I come up from San Salvador this morning to close the deal, the Sun Bank in Miami is supposed to have the telex, the Sun Bank in Miami does not have the telex. Now I ask you, Mr. Lee. Please. What am I supposed to do?

The man slammed down the phone.

The gray-haired woman took a San Salvador newspaper from her Vuitton tote and began reading it.

The man stared balefully at Elena.

Elena shifted her gaze, a hedge against the possibility that eye contact could be construed as standing out. Across the room a steward was watching *General Hospital* on the television set above the bar.

She heard the man again punching numbers into the telephone but did not look at him.

Mr. Lee, the man said.

A silence.

Elena allowed her eyes to wander. The headline on the paper the woman was reading was GOBIERNO VENDE 85% LECHE DONADA.

All right, the man said. You are not Mr. Lee. My mistake. But if you are truly the son you are also Mr.

Lee. So let me speak to your father, Mr. Lee. What is this, he cannot come to the phone? I am talking to him, he tells me to call back in ten minutes. I am calling back from a pay phone in the Miami airport and he cannot take the call? What is this? Mr. Lee. Please. I am getting from you both a bunch of lies. A bunch of misinformation. Disinformation. Lies. Mr. Lee. Listen to me. It costs me maybe a million dollars to put you and your father out of business, believe me, I will spend it.

Again the phone was slammed down.

GOBIERNO VENDE 85% LECHE DONADA. The government sells eighty-five percent of donated milk. It struck Elena that her Spanish must have failed, this was too broad to be an accurate translation.

Elena did not yet know how broad a story could get.

Again the man punched in numbers. Mr. Elman. Let me tell you the situation here. I am calling from a pay phone in the Miami airport. I fly up from San Salvador today. Because today the deal was to close. Today the Sun Bank in Miami would have the telex to approve the line of credit. Today the Sun Bank in Miami does not have the telex. Today I am sitting in the Miami airport and I don't know what to do. That is the situation here. Okay, Mr. Elman. We have a little problem here, which I'm sure we can solve.

The calls continued. Mr. Lee. Mr. Elman. Mr. Gordon. Someone was in Toronto and someone else was in Los Angeles and many people were in Miami. At four o'clock Elena heard the door buzz. At the moment she allowed herself to look up she saw Barry Sedlow, without breaking stride as he walked toward her, lay an envelope on the table next to the telephone the Salvadoran was using.

"Here is my concern," the Salvadoran was saying into the telephone as he fingered the envelope. "Mr. Elman. You and I, we have *confianza*." The Salvadoran placed the envelope in an inner pocket of his silk jacket. "But what I am being fed from Mr. Lee is a bunch of disinformation."

Later in Barry Sedlow's car on the way to Hialeah she had asked who the Salvadoran was.

"What made you think he was Salvadoran," Barry Sedlow said.

She told him.

"Lot of people say they came up from San Salvador this morning, lot of people read Salvadoran papers, that doesn't make them Salvadoran."

She asked what the man was if not Salvadoran.

"I didn't say he wasn't Salvadoran," Barry Sedlow said. "Did I. You have a bad habit of jumping to conclusions." In the silence that followed he slowed to a stop at an intersection, reached inside the Dolphins warm-up jacket he was wearing and took aim at the streetlight.

One thing she had learned growing up around her father: she recognized guns.

The gun Barry Sedlow had taken from inside his warm-up jacket was a 9mm Browning with sound suppressor.

The engine was idling and the sound of the silenced shot inaudible.

The light shattered and the intersection went dark.

"Transit passenger," Barry Sedlow had said as he transferred his foot from brake to accelerator. "Already on the six-thirty back to San Sal. Not our deal." When I say that Elena was not one of those who saw how every moment could connect I mean that it did not occur to her that a transit passenger need show no visa.

Cast your mind back.

Refresh your memory if necessary: go to Nexis, go to microfiche.

Try to locate the most interesting news stories of the period in question.

Scroll past any stories that led or even made the evening news.

Move down instead until you locate the kind of two-inch wire story that tended to appear just under the page-fourteen continuation of the page-one story on congressional response to the report of the Kissinger Commission, say, or opposite the page-nineteen continuation of the page-one story about the federal court ruling upholding investigation of possible violations of the Neutrality Act.

The kind of two-inch wire story that had to do with chartered aircraft of uncertain ownership that did or did not leave one or another southern airport loaded with one or another kind of cargo.

Many manifests were eventually analyzed by those who followed such stories.

Many personnel records were eventually accessed.

Many charts were eventually drawn detailing the ways in which the spectral companies with the high-concept names (*Amalgamated Commercial Enterprises Inc., Defex S.A., Energy Resources International*) tended to interlock.

These two-inch aircraft stories were not always identical. In some stories the aircraft in question was reported not to have left one or another southern airport but to have crashed in Georgia or experienced mechanical difficulties in Texas or been seized in the Bahamas in relation to one or another narcotics investigation. Nor was the cargo in these stories always identical: inspection of the cargo revealed in some cases an unspecified number of reconditioned Soviet AK-47s, in other cases unspecified numbers of M67 fragmentation grenades, AR-15s, M-60s, RPG-7 rocket launchers, boxes of ammo, pallets of POMZ-2 fragmentation mines, British Aerospace L-9 antitank mines, Chinese Type 72A and Italian Valmara 69 antipersonnel mines.

69s.

Epperson had floated a figure of three dollars per for 69s and now he was claiming the market had dropped to two per.

I'm not sure I know what business Epperson is in.

Christ, what business are they all in.

Some people in Washington said that the flights described in these stories were not occurring, other people in Washington (more careful people in Washington, more specific people in Washington, people in Washington who did not intend to perjure themselves when the hearings rolled in) said that the flights *could not be* occurring, or *could only be* occurring, *if indeed they were* occurring, outside the range of possible knowledge.

I myself learned to be specific during this period.

I myself learned to be careful.

I myself learned the art of the conditional.

I recall asking Treat Morrison, during the course of my preliminary interviews with him at his office in Washington, *if* in fact, *to his knowledge*, anyone in the United States government *could have* knowledge that *one or more* such flights *could be* supplying arms to the so-called contra forces for the purpose of over-throwing the Sandinista government in Nicaragua.

There had been a silence.

Treat Morrison had picked up a pen and put it down.

I flattered myself that I was on the edge of something revelatory.

"To the extent that the area in question touches on the lake," Treat Morrison said, "and to the extent that the lake has been historically construed as our lake, it goes without saying that we could have an interest. However."

Again he fell silent.

I waited.

We had gotten as far as claiming the Caribbean as our lake, our sea, *mare nostrum.*

"However," Treat Morrison repeated.

I debated with myself whether I would accept an off-the-record or not-for-attribution stipulation.

"We don't track that kind of activity," Treat Morrison said then.

One of those flights that no one was tracking lifted off from Fort Lauderdale–Hollywood International Airport at one-thirty on the morning of June 26 1984. The aircraft was a Lockheed L-100. The official documents filed by the pilot showed a crew of five, two passengers, a cargo of assorted auto parts, and the destination San José, Costa Rica.

The U.S. Customs official who certified the manifest did not elect to physically inspect the cargo.

The plane did not land in San José, Costa Rica.

The plane had no reason to land in San José, Costa Rica, because an alternative infrastructure was already in place: the eight-thousand-foot runways laid by the 46th Combat Engineers during the aftermath of the Big Pine II maneuvers were already in place. The radar sites were in place. The water purification and delivery systems were in place. "You got yourself a regular little piece of U.S.A. here," the pilot of the Lockheed L-100 said to Elena McMahon as they waited on the dry grass off the runway while the cargo was unloaded.

"Actually I'll be going right back." She felt a sudden need to distance herself from whatever was going on here. "I mean I left my car at the airport."

"Long-term parking I hope," the pilot said.

What was also in place was the deal.

We don't track that kind of activity.

No comment. Thank you. Goodbye.

Two

Two

I

The persona of "the writer" does not attract me. As a way of being it has its flat sides. Nor am I comfortable around the literary life: its traditional dramatic line (the romance of solitude, of interior struggle, of the lone seeker after truth) came to seem early on a trying conceit. I lost patience somewhat later with the conventions of the craft, with exposition, with transitions, with the development and revelation of "character." To this point I recall my daughter's resistance when asked, in the eighth grade at the Westlake School for Girls in Los Angeles, to write an "autobiographical" essay (*your life, age thirteen, thesis, illustration, summary, just try it, no more than two double-spaced pages neatly typed please*) on whatever event or individual or experience had "most changed" her life. I mentioned a few of the applicable perennials (trip to Europe, volunteer job in hospital, teacher she didn't like because he made her work too hard and then it turned out to be worth it), she, less facile, less careful, more sentient, mentioned the death of her best friend in fourth grade.

Yes, I said, ashamed. Better. You have it.

"Not really," she said.

Why not, I said.

"Because it didn't actually change my life. I mean I cried, I was sad, I wrote a lot about it in my diary, yes, but what changed?"

I recall explaining that "change" was merely the convention at hand: I said that while it was true that the telling of a life tended to falsify it, gave it a form it did not intrinsically possess, this was just a fact of writing things down, something we all accepted.

I realized as I was saying this that I no longer did.

I realized that I was increasingly interested only in the technical, in how to lay down the AM-2 aluminum matting for the runway, in whether or not parallel taxiways and high-speed turnoffs must be provided, in whether an eight-thousand-foot runway requires sixty thousand square yards of operational apron or only forty thousand. If the AM-2 is laid directly over laterite instead of over plastic membrane seal, how long would we have before base failure results? (How long would we *need* before base failure results was another question altogether, one I left to the Treat Morrisons of this world.) How large a base camp will a fifteen-hundred-kilowatt generator service? In the absence of high-capacity deep wells, can water be effectively treated with tactical erdlators? I give you Friedrich Wilhelm Nietzsche, 1844–1900: "When man does not have firm, calm lines on the horizon of his life—mountain and forest lines, as it were—then man's most inner will becomes agitated, preoccupied and wistful."

Tactical erdlators have been my mountain and forest lines.

This business of Elena McMahon, then, is hard for me.

This business of what "changed" her, what "motivated" her, what made her do it.

I see her standing in the dry grass off the runway, her arms bare, her sunglasses pushed up into her loose hair, her black silk shift wrinkled from the flight, and wonder what made her think a black silk shift bought off a sale rack at Bergdorf Goodman during the New York primary was the appropriate thing to wear on an unscheduled cargo flight at one-thirty in the morning out of Fort Lauderdale–Hollywood International Airport, destination San José Costa Rica but not quite.

Her sunglasses are pushed up but her eyes are shut tight.

A dog (underfed, mangy, of no remarkable size) is bursting from the open door of a concrete structure off the apron and racing toward her.

The man beside her, his head shaved, cutoff jeans slung below his navel, is singing the theme from *Bonanza* as he crouches and beckons to the dog.

> *We got a right to pick a little fight —*
> *Bo-nan-za—*
> *If anyone fights with any one of us —*
> *He's got a fight with me —*

Her eyes remain shut.

On second thought I am not sure what would be, in this context, "appropriate."

Possibly the baseball cap lent her by one of the refueling crew. The cap was lettered NBC SPORTS, its familiar peacock logo smeared with diesel fuel.

"Actually I think somebody was supposed to meet

me," she said to the pilot when the man with the shaved head had disappeared and the last pallet been unloaded and the refueling completed. Over the past dozen hours she had come to see the pilot as her partner, her backup, her protection, her single link to the day before.

"Looks like somebody didn't give you the full skinny," the pilot said.

Smell of jasmine, pool of blue jacaranda.

Coincidentally, although not really, since it was in the role of mother that I first knew Elena, Catherine Janklow was also in that eighth-grade class at the Westlake School for Girls in Los Angeles. Elena's performance as a Westlake Mom (so we were called in school bulletins) was so attentive to detail as to be impenetrable. She organized benefits for the scholarship fund, opened her house for picnics and ditch days and sleepovers, got up every Friday at four hours before dawn to deliver the Astronomy Club to remote starwatching locations in Lancaster or Latigo Canyon or the Santa Susana Mountains, and was duly repaid by the attendance of three eighth graders at her Westlake Career Day workshop on "Getting Started as a Reporter."

"You're at an age right now when it's impossible even to imagine how much your life is going to change," Elena told the three eighth graders who turned up for her Career Day workshop.

Two of the eighth graders maintained expressions of polite disbelief.

The third jabbed a finger into the air, then crossed her arms truculently across her chest.

Elena looked at the child. Her name was Melissa

Simon. She was Mort Simon's daughter. Mort Simon was someone Wynn knew who had improved the year by taking a motion picture studio private and spinning off its real assets into various of his personal companies.

"Melissa."

"Excuse me," Melissa Simon said. "But I don't quite see why my life is supposed to change."

There had been a silence.

"That's an interesting point," Elena had said then.

Catherine had not attended her mother's workshop on Getting Started as a Reporter. Catherine had signed up for a workshop conducted by a Westlake Mom who happened to be a business affairs lawyer at Paramount ("Motion Picture Development—Where Do You Fit In?"), then skipped it to finish her own eighth-grade autobiographical essay on the event or individual or experience that had "most changed" her life. "What is definitely most changing my life this semester is my mother getting cancer," Catherine's autobiographical essay began, and continued for two neatly typed double-spaced pages. Catherine's mother, according to Catherine, was that semester "too tired to do anything normal" because every morning after dropping the car pool at school she had been going to UCLA for what Catherine knowledgeably described as "radiation zapping following the exsishun [sic] of a stage 1 good prognose [sic] breast lesion." That this was not a fact generally known does not, to me, suggest "motivation."

Treat Morrison knew it, because he recognized the scar.

Diane had had the same scar.

Look, he said when Elena fell silent. What difference does it make. You get it one way or you get it another, nobody comes through free.

She sat on the dry grass in her black silk shift and the cap lettered NBC SPORTS and watched the L-100 taxi out for takeoff and tried to think what to do next. The cargo had been loaded onto flatbed trucks. Whoever was supposed to make the payment had not appeared. She had thought at first that the man with the shaved head and the cutoff jeans was her contact but he was not. He was, he said, on his way home to Tulsa from Angola. He was, he said, just lending a little expertise while he was in this particular area.

She had not asked him how this particular area could reasonably be construed as on the way to Tulsa from Angola.

She had not asked him what expertise he was lending.

During the ten minutes she had spent trying to talk the pilot into waiting for her contact the flatbed trucks had been driven away.

She was going to need to rethink this step by step.

She was going to need to reconnoiter, reassess.

The L-100 and the zone of safety it represented were about to vanish into the cloud cover.

Fly it down, fly it back, the pilot had said. That's my contract. I get paid to drive the bus. I get paid to drive the bus when the engines are overheating. I get paid to drive the bus when the loran goes down. I don't get paid to take care of the passengers.

Her partner, her backup, her protection.

Her single link to the day before.

He had flown it down and now he was flying it back.

Per his contract.

She did not think it possible that her father would find himself in exactly this situation, yet she had done exactly what he said he had to do. She had done exactly what her father said he had to do and she had done exactly what Barry Sedlow said to do.

Just do it my way for a change.

This would very soon be all right.

She would very soon know what to do.

She felt alert, a little light-headed. She did not yet know where she was, and the clearing in which the strip had been laid down had suddenly cleared of people, but she was ready, open to information.

This should be Costa Rica.

If this was Costa Rica the first thing she needed to do was get to San José.

She did not know what she would do if she did get to San José but there would be a hotel, offices of American banks, an airport with scheduled carriers.

Through the open door of the concrete structure off the apron she could see, intermittently, someone moving, someone walking around, a man, a man with a ponytail, a man with a ponytail wearing fatigues. She kept her eyes on this door and tried to recall lessons learned in other venues, other vocations. One thing she had learned during her four-year sojourn at the *Herald Examiner* was how easy it was to get into places where no one was supposed to be. The trick was to attach oneself to service personnel, people who had no particular investment in who got in and who stayed out. She had on one occasion followed a telephone crew into a locked hangar in which an experimental stealth bomber was being readied for its first rollout. She had on more than one occasion gotten inside a house where someone did not want to talk to her by striking up conversation with the pool man, the gardener, the dog groomer who had run a cord inside the kitchen door to plug in a dryer.

In fact she had mentioned this during the course of her Westlake Career Day workshop.

Melissa Simon had again raised her hand. She had a point she wanted to make. The point she wanted to make was that "nobody from the media could have ever gotten into those houses if the families had normal security and their public relations people were doing their job."

Which had prompted Elena to raise the Westlake Career Day stakes exponentially by suggesting, in words that either did or did not include the phrase "try living in the real world for a change," that very few families in the world outside three or four well-defined neighborhoods on the West Side of Los Angeles County had either public relations people or what one very fortunate eighth grader might call "normal security."

Which had caused Wynn Janklow, after this was reported to him the next day by three different people (Mort Simon's partner, Mort Simon's lawyer, and the young woman who was described as Mort Simon's "issues person"), to leave half his lunch at Hillcrest uneaten in order to call Elena.

"I hear you've been telling our friends' kids their parents live in a dream world."

In the first place, she said, this was not an exact quotation.

He said something else but the connection was bad.

In the second place, she said, Mort Simon was not her friend. She didn't even know Mort Simon.

Wynn was calling from his Mercedes, driving east on Pico, and had turned up Robertson before his voice faded back in.

"You want everybody in town saying you talk like a shiksa," he had said, "you're getting the job done."

"I am a shiksa," she had said.

"That's your problem, not mine," he had said.

In fact she did khow Mort Simon.

Of course she knew Mort Simon.

The house in Beverly Hills where she sat on the sidewalk waiting for the pool report on the celebrity fundraiser was as it happened Mort Simon's house. She had even seen him briefly, lifting a transparent flap of the Regal Rents tent to survey the barricade behind which the press was waiting. He had looked directly at her but such was his generalized view of the world outside his tent that he had not recognized her and she had not spoken.

"Send out some refreshments," she had heard him say to a waiter before he dropped the flap, although no refreshments ever materialized. "Like, you know, diet Pepsi, water, I'm not paying so they can tank up."

The wife and daughter no longer lived in the house. The wife and daughter had moved to a town house just inside the Beverly Hills line from Century City and the daughter had transferred from Westlake to Beverly Hills High School. Catherine had told her that.

Living in the real world.

We had a real life and now we don't.

She put that out of her mind.

Other lessons.

More recent venues.

Not long after moving to Washington she had interviewed an expert on nuclear security who had explained how easy it would be to score plutonium. The security for nuclear facilities, he said, was always contracted out. The contractors in turn hired locally and supplied their hires with minimum rounds of ammunition. Meaning, he had said, "you got multimillion-dollar state-of-the-art security systems being operated by downsized sheriff's deputies with maybe enough ammo to take down a coyote."

She remembered exactly what he said because the interview had ended up in the Sunday magazine and this had been the pull quote.

If she could think of the man with the ponytail as a downsized sheriff's deputy, a downsized sheriff's deputy lacking even a multimillion-dollar state-of-the-art security system, this would be all right.

All it would take was nerve.

All it would take was a show of belonging wherever it was she wanted to be.

She got up, brushed the grass off her legs and walked to the open door of the concrete structure off the apron. The man with the ponytail was seated at a wooden crate on which there was an electric fan, a bottle of beer and a worn deck of Bicycle cards. He drained the beer, lobbed the bottle into a metal drum, and, with two fingers held stiff, turned over a card.

"Shit," the man said, then looked up.

"You're supposed to see that I get to San José," she said. "They were supposed to have told you that."

The man turned over another card. "Who was supposed to tell me that."

82

This was going to require more work than the average telephone crew, pool man, dog groomer.

"If I don't get to San José they're going to be wondering why."

"Who is."

She gambled. "I think you know who."

"Give me a name."

She had not been given names. She had asked Barry Sedlow for names and he had talked about compartmentalization, cutouts, need-to-know.

You wouldn't give me their real names anyway, she had said. Just give me the names they use.

What's that supposed to mean, he had said.

The names they use like you use Gary Barnett, she had said.

I'm not authorized to give you that information, he had said. Somebody's supposed to meet you. Your need-to-know stops there.

Somebody was supposed to meet her but somebody did not meet her.

Somebody was supposed to make the payment and somebody had not made the payment.

She was aware as she watched the man turn over cards of a sudden darkening outside, then of lightning. There was a map of Costa Rica on the wall of the concrete structure, reinforcing the impression that this was Costa Rica but offering no clue as to where in Costa Rica. The overhead light flickered and went out. The electric fan fluttered to a stop. In the absence of background noise she realized that she had been hearing the whine of an overworked refrigerator, now silent.

The man with the ponytail got up, opened the refrigerator, and took another beer from its darkened interior. He did not offer one to Elena. Instead he sat down and turned over another card, whistling softly between his teeth, as if Elena were invisible.

Who is.

I think you know who.

Give me a name.

"Epperson," she said. She seized the name from the ether of the past ten days. "Max Epperson."

The man with the ponytail looked at her, then shuffled the cards and got up. "I could be overdue a night or two in Josie," the man said.

2

W hen I am away from this I tend to elongate the time sequence, which was in fact quite short. It was early on the morning of June 26 1984 when Elena McMahon left Fort Lauderdale–Hollywood International Airport on the L-100, and late the same morning when the L-100 landed somewhere in Costa Rica. It was close to midnight of the same day (first there had been a bridge washed out, then a two-hour stop parked outside what seemed to be a military installation) when Elena McMahon got to San José. *You're* doing nothing, the man with the ponytail had said when she asked what they were doing at the military installation. What *I'm* doing doesn't concern you.

He had gotten out of the truck.

Anyone asks, he had said, tell them you're waiting for Mr. Jones.

From the time he reappeared two hours later until they reached San José he had not spoken. He had instead sung to himself, repeated fragments of what appeared to be the same song, so inaudibly that she knew he was singing only by the periodic spasms of pounding on the steering wheel as he exhaled the words "*great balls* of fire." In San José he had driven directly to a hotel on what appeared to be a downtown side street. Free ride ends here, he had said. Seen from the unlit street the hotel had an impressive glass porte cochere and polished brass letters reading HOTEL COLONIAL but once she was inside the small lobby the promise faded. There was no air-conditioning. An industrial fluorescent light flickered overhead, casting a sickly light on the stained velour upholstery of the single chair. As she waited for the desk clerk to finish a telephone call she had begun to find it inauspicious that the man with the ponytail had brought her to this hotel without ever asking where she wanted to go (in fact she would have had no idea where to go, she had never before been in San José), just pulled directly under the porte cochere and stopped, letting the engine idle as he waited for her to get out.

Why here, she had asked.

Why not here. He had flicked his headlights off and on several times. I thought you wanted to run into people you know.

There was a pay telephone on the wall by the elevator.

She would call Barry Sedlow.

The first thing to do was get in touch with Barry Sedlow.

As she opened her bag and tried to locate the card on which he had written the 800 number for his beeper she became aware of the desk clerk watching her.

She would tell the desk clerk she needed a drugstore, a doctor, a *clínica*.

She would get out of this place.

She had seen a bus station on the way to the hotel,

the bus station would be open, she could make the call from the bus station.

She did not bother to remember the directions the desk clerk gave her to the *clínica* but as it happened she passed it on her way to the bus station. That at least was good. This could be going her way. In case anyone was watching she had been walking toward the *clínica*.

The bus station was almost deserted.

The dispatcher was sleeping noisily in a metal cage above the concourse.

The public telephones in the waiting room had rotary dials and could not be used to leave a message on a beeper, which was the only number she had for Barry Sedlow. *Emergencia,* she said over and over when she managed to wake the dispatcher. She held out a ten-dollar bill and the KROME GUN CLUB card on which Barry Sedlow had written the 800 number. *La clínica. Mi padre.* The dispatcher examined the bill and the card, then dialed the number on his push-button phone and left as a callback number one of the public phones in the waiting room.

She sat on a molded plastic bench and drank a local cola, sweet and warm and flat, and waited for the phone to ring.

Don't get your balls in an uproar, Barry Sedlow said when she picked up the phone. You made the delivery, you'll get the payment. Sometimes these things take a little longer, you got a whole bureaucracy you're dealing with, they got requisitions, regulations, paperwork, special ways they have to do things, they don't just peel off cash like guys on the street. Be smart. Stay put. I'll make a few calls, get back to you. You cool?

All right, she had said finally.

By the way, he had said then. I wouldn't call your dad. I'm keeping him in the picture about where you are and what you're doing, but I wouldn't call him.

It would not have occurred to her to call her father but she asked why not.

Because it wouldn't be smart, he had said. I'll get back to you at the Colonial.

It was almost dawn, after she had gone back to the Hotel Colonial and let the desk clerk take her passport and run her credit card, after she had gone upstairs to the single room on the third floor and sat on the edge of the metal bed and abandoned the idea of sleep, before it occurred to her that during the call to Barry Sedlow she had never once mentioned the name of the hotel.

So what, Barry Sedlow said when he finally called back and she put this to him.

Big fucking deal. Where else would you be.

This second conversation with Barry Sedlow took place on the afternoon of June 28. It was the evening of July 1 when Barry Sedlow called the third time. It was the morning of July 2 when, using the commercial ticket provided her, a one-way nonexchangeable ticket to a designated destination, Elena McMahon left San José for the island where the incident occurred that should not have occurred.

Should not have occurred and could not have been predicted.

By any quantitative measurement.

3

You will have noticed that I am not giving you the name of this island.

This is deliberate, a decision on my part, and not a decision (other writers have in fact named the island, for example, the authors of the Rand study) based on classification.

The name would get in the way.

If you knew the name you might recall days or nights spent on this island en route to or in lieu of more desirable islands, the metallic taste of tinned juice in rum punches, the mosquitoes under the net at night, the rented villa where the septic tank backed up, the unpleasantness over the Jet Ski misunderstanding, the hours spent waiting in the jammed airport when the scheduled Windward Air or BIWI flights failed to materialize, the piece of needlepoint you meant to finish and instead spotted with coconut oil, the book you meant to read and distractedly set aside, the tedium of all forlorn tropical places.

The determined resistance to gravity, the uneasy reduction of the postcolonial dilemma to the Jet Ski misunderstanding.

The guilty pleasure of buckling in and clearing the ground and knowing that you will step off this plane in the developed world.

Little guessing that the pleasant life of the plantations was about to disappear, as the history of the island you dutifully bought at the airport puts it. *Paradisaical as the sight of land must have been after the long voyage from the Cape Verdes. Not to overlook the contribution made by early Jewish settlers after the construction of their historic crushed-coral synagogue, so situated as to offer a noteworthy view of Rum Cay. Signalling a resounding defeat for the Party that had spearheaded the movement toward The Independence.*

Face it.

You did not, during your sojourns on this island, want to know its history. (High points: Arawaks, hurricane, sugar, Middle Passage, the abandonment known as The Independence.) You did not, if you had planned well, have reason to frequent its major city. (Must see: that historic crushed-coral synagogue, its noteworthy view of Rum Cay.) You had no need to venture beyond the rust-stained but still daunting (school of Edward Durell Stone) facade of our embassy there. Had you discovered such need (bad planning, trouble, a lost passport), you would have found it a larger embassy than extant American interests on the island would seem to require, a relic of the period when Washington had been gripped by the notion that the emergence of independent nations on single-crop islands with annual per capita incomes in three digits offered the exact optimum conditions under which private capital could be siphoned off the Asian rim and into *mare nostrum*.

Many phantom investment schemes had been encouraged on this island. Many training sessions had been planned, many promotional tours staged. Many pilot programs had been undertaken, each cited at its inception as a flawless model of how a responsible superpower could help bring an LDC, or Lesser Developed Country, into the roster of the self-sufficient NICs, or New Industrializing Countries. On an island where most human concerns were obliterated by weather, this was an embassy in which tropical doubts had been held at bay via the mastery of acronyms.

It was still in 1984 possible to hear in this embassy about "CBMs," or Confidence Building Measures.

It was still in 1984 possible to hear about "BHN," or Basic Human Needs.

What could not be obfuscated by acronym tended to be reduced to its most cryptic diminutive. I recall hearing at this embassy a good deal about "the Del" before I learned that it referred to a formula for predicting events developed by the Rand Corporation and less jauntily known as the Delphi Method (that which should not have happened and could not have been predicted by any quantitative measurement had presumably not been predicted by employment of the Del), and I sat through an entire study group session on "Ap Tech—Uses and Misuses" before I divined that the topic at hand was something called the Appropriate Technology movement, proponents of which apparently did not believe that technology developed in the first world was appropriate for transfer to the third. I recall heated discussion on whether the introduction of data processing into the island's literacy program either could or could not be construed as Ap Tech. Tech skills are in a different basket, an economic attaché kept repeating. Tech skills are a basket-two priority. A series of political appointees, retired contributors from the intermountain West, had passed in and out of the official residence without ever finding need to master the particular dialect spoken in this embassy.

Alexander Brokaw was of course not a political appointee.

Alex Brokaw was career, with a c.v. of sensitive postings.

Alex Brokaw had arrived on this island six months before to do a specific job.

A job that entailed bringing in the pros.

Because, as Alex Brokaw often said, *if and when this switches gear into a full-scale effort, we'll be rotating troops in and out, which is good for home-front morale but not good for construction continuity. So we damn well better bring the pros in up front.*

The pros and of course the Special Forces guys.

A job that entailed establishing the presence on the island of this selected group of Americans, and discouraging the presence of all others.

Which is why Alex Brokaw mentioned to his DCM, after the incident at the embassy's Fourth of July picnic, that it might be useful to run a background on Elise Meyer, which was the name on the passport Elena McMahon was by then using.

4

When I try to understand how Elena McMahon could have assimilated with no perceptible beat the logic of traveling on a passport not her own to a place she had no previous intention of going, could have accepted so readily that radical revision of who she was, could have walked into a life not her own and lived it, I consider the last time I actually saw her.

Academy Award night, 1982.

When she was still living in the house on the Pacific Coast Highway.

It was five months later when she walked out of that house and enrolled Catherine at an Episcopal boarding school in Rhode Island and got herself hired (on the basis not of her long-gone four-year career at the *Herald Examiner* but of an editorial hunch that Wynn Janklow's scrupulously bilateral campaign contributions might still buy his estranged wife some access) at the Washington *Post*.

All that happened very fast.

All that happened so fast that the first I knew of it was when I got home from France in September of

1982 and began to go through the accumulated mail and was about to discard unopened, because it looked like one or another plea in support of or opposition to one or another issue, a plain white envelope with metered postage and a Washington D.C. return address. Had I not been distracted by a phone call I would never have opened the envelope, but I was, and I did, and there it was: a handwritten note, signed *Elena*, saying that of course I already knew that she and Catherine had relocated to the East Coast but now she was settled and just getting around to sending out her address. The printed name on the change-of-address card clipped to the note was *Elena McMahon*.

"Relocated" was the word she used.

As if leaving Wynn Janklow had been a corporate transfer.

I had not already known that she and Catherine had relocated to the East Coast.

I had known nothing.

All I knew was that on Academy Award night that year Elena McMahon had still been Elena Janklow, sitting in front of a plate of untouched cassoulet at the party that was in our rather insular community at that time the single event approaching a command performance, absently twining a Mylar ribbon torn from a balloon into the rhinestone strap of her dress. I never once saw her look at the big television screens mounted at every eye line, not even at those moments when a local favorite was up for an award and the party fell momentarily silent. Nor did she observe the other core tribal custom of the evening, which was to spring up and move toward the bar as soon as the awards ended, allowing the tables to be cleared while applauding both the triumphant arrivals of the winners and the inspirational sportsmanship of the losers.

Elena never got up at all.

Elena stayed seated, idly picking apart a table decoration to remove the miniature Oscar at its center, oblivious to winners and losers alike, oblivious even to the busboys changing the tablecloth in front of her. Only when I sat down across the table did she even look up.

"I promised Catherine," she said about the miniature Oscar.

What she said next that Academy Award night was something I interpreted at the time to mean only that she was tired of the event's structural festivity, that she had been dressed up in rhinestones in broad daylight since four in the afternoon and sitting at this table since five and now she wanted to go home.

I was wrong about what she said next.

As I would be wrong later to wonder how she could so readily assimilate the logic of walking into a life not her own and living it.

What she said next that Academy Award night was this: "I can't fake this anymore."

Suggesting that she had assimilated that logic a long time before.

5

"Somebody's going to let you know the move they want you to make," Barry Sedlow had said the last time he called her in San José.

"When," she had said.

"By the way. I saw your dad. He says hi. I'm keeping him in the picture."

Saying "hi" was not in her father's vocabulary but she let this go. "I asked when."

"Just stay put."

In the six days since her arrival in San José she had left the room at the Colonial only twice, once to buy a toothbrush and a tin of aspirin, the second time to buy a T-shirt and cotton pants so that she could wash the black silk shift. She had given the maid American dollars to bring back sandwiches, coffee, once in a while a Big Mac from the McDonald's across from the bus station.

"That's what you told me the night I got here. I've *been* staying put. I need to know when."

"Hard to say. Maybe tonight." There had been a silence. "They may want you to take payment in another venue. Who knows."

"Where."

"They'll let you know where."

An hour later the envelope containing the passport and plane ticket had begun to appear, emerging at such barely perceptible speed that she was finally forced to breathe, under the locked door of her room at the Colonial.

She did not know why she had happened to look at the door at the very moment the envelope began to appear.

There had been no giveaway sound, no rustle of paper on carpet, no fumbling in the corridor.

The envelope had been clear of the door and lying motionless inside the room for a full five minutes before, still frozen, she moved to approach it. The ticket bearing the name Elise Meyer had been written by American Airlines in Miami on June 30 1984. The passport bearing the name Elise Meyer had been issued on June 30 1984 at the United States Passport Agency in Miami.

In the photograph affixed to this passport she was smiling.

In the photograph affixed to her own passport she was not.

She could not compare the two because her own passport was downstairs in the hotel safe, but she was quite certain that the photographs were otherwise similar.

She studied the photograph on the passport for some time before she sorted out how it could happen to be otherwise similar to the photograph on her own passport. It could happen to be otherwise similar to the photograph on her own passport because it had been taken at the same time, not long after she got to

97

Washington, in a passport-photo place across from the paper. She had asked for extra Polaroids to use for visas. At some point recently on this campaign (whenever it was that the Secret Service had come on and started demanding photos for new credentials) she had stuck the five or six remaining prints in a pocket of her computer bag.

Why wouldn't she have.

Of course she did.

Of course her computer bag was in a closet at the house in Sweetwater.

By the way. I saw your dad. He says hi. I'm keeping him in the picture.

6

Of course Dick McMahon was by then dead. Of course he had died under circumstances that would not appear in the least out of order: the notification to the nursing agency at noon on June 27 that Mr. McMahon's night shift would no longer be required; the predictable midnight emergency twelve hours later; the fortuitous and virtually simultaneous arrival at the house in Sweetwater of the very attentive young doctor; the transfer in the early morning hours of June 28 to the two-bed room at the Clearview Convalescent Lodge in South Kendall; the flurry of visits over the next thirty-six hours from the very attentive young doctor and then the certification of the death.

It would not be unusual at this facility to see a degree of agitation in a new admission.

Nor would it be unusual, given the extreme agitation of this new admission, if a decision were made to increase sedation.

Nor would it be unusual, given the continuing attempts of this extremely agitated new admission to initiate contact with the patient in the other bed, to effect the temporary transfer of the patient in the other bed to a more comfortable gurney in the staff smoking lounge.

Nor would it be unusual if such an extremely agitated and increasingly ill new admission were, the best efforts of his very attentive young doctor notwithstanding, to just go. "Just going" was how dying was characterized at the Clearview Convalescent Lodge, by both patients and staff. He's just going. He just went.

Nor would there be need for an autopsy, because whatever happened would be certified as having happened in a licensed care facility under the care of a licensed physician.

There would be nothing out of order about the certification.

Without question Dick McMahon would be gone by the time he was certified dead.

Which was, according to the records of the Clearview Convalescent Lodge in South Kendall, at 1:23 a.m. on the morning of June 30. Since certification occurred after midnight the bill submitted for reimbursement under Medicare A was for three full nights, June 28, 29 and 30. *Policyholder deceased 171.4* was the notation placed on the Medicare A billing in the space provided for Full Description of Condition at Discharge Including Diagnostic Code.

McMAHON, Richard Allen: age 74, died under care of physician June 30, 1984, at Clearview Convalescent Lodge, South Kendall. No services are scheduled.

So read the agate-type notice appearing in the vital statistics column, which was compiled daily to include those deaths and births and marriages entered into the previous day's public record, of the July 2 1984 edition of the Miami *Herald*.

It could have been established, by anyone who cared to check the nursing agency's file on Mr. McMahon, that the June 27 call ordering the cancellation of Mr. McMahon's night shift had been placed by a woman identifying herself as Mr. McMahon's daughter.

It would remain unestablished who had placed the midnight call to the very attentive young doctor.

Because no one asked.

Because the single person who might have asked had not yet had the opportunity to read the agate-type notice appearing in the vital statistics column of the July 2 1984 edition of the Miami *Herald*.

Because the single person who might have asked did not yet know that her father was dead.

By the way. I wouldn't call your dad. I'm keeping him in the picture about where you are and what you're doing, but I wouldn't call him.

Because it wouldn't be smart.

7

At the time she left San José she did not yet know that her father was dead but there were certain things she did already know. Some of what she already knew at the time she left San José she had learned before she ever got to Costa Rica, had known in fact since the afternoon the sky went dark and the lightning forked on the horizon outside Dick McMahon's room at Jackson Memorial and he began to tell her who it was he had to see and what it was he had to do. Some of what she already knew she had learned the day she brought him home from Jackson Memorial to the house in Sweetwater and managed to deflect his intention to drive down to where the *Kitty Rex* was berthed and Barry Sedlow was waiting for him. Some of what she already knew she believed to be true and some of what she already knew she believed to be delusion, but since this was a business in which truth and delusion appeared equally doubtful she was left to proceed as if even the most apparently straightforward piece of information could at any time explode.

Any piece of information was a potential fragmentation mine.

Fragmentation mines came immediately to mind because of one of the things she already knew.

This was one of the things she already knew: the shipment on the L-100 that left Fort Lauderdale–Hollywood International Airport at one-thirty on the morning of June 26 was composed exclusively of fragmentation mines, three hundred and twenty-four pallets, each pallet loaded with twelve crates, each crate containing between ten and two hundred mines depending upon their type and size. Some of these mines were antitank and some antipersonnel. There were the forty-seven-inch L-9 antitanks made by British Aerospace and there were the thirteen-inch PT-MI-BA III antitanks made by the Czechs. There were the POMZ-2 antipersonnels and there were the Chinese Type 72A antipersonnels and there were the Italian Valmara 69 antipersonnels.

69s.

Epperson had floated a figure of three dollars per for 69s and now he was claiming the market had dropped to two per.

When the pallets of 69s had finally been unloaded on the runway that morning she had been handed a hammer by the man with the shaved head and cutoff jeans and told to open a crate so that he could verify the merchandise.

Open it yourself, she had said, offering him back the hammer.

It doesn't work that way, he had said, not taking the hammer.

She had hesitated.

He had unknotted a T-shirt from his belt and pulled it over his bare chest. The T-shirt was printed with an American flag and the legend THESE COLORS DON'T RUN.

I got nowhere particular to go, he had said, so it's your call.

She had pried open the crate and indicated the contents.

He had extracted one of the small plastic devices, examined it, walked away and placed it on the ground halfway between Elena and the concrete structure. When he returned to Elena he was singing tunelessly, snatches of the theme from *Bonanza*.

He had moved back, and motioned her to do the same.

Then he had aimed a remote at the plastic device and whistled.

When she saw the dog burst from the open door of the concrete structure she had closed her eyes. The explosion had occurred between *We got a right to pick a little fight* and *Bo-nan-za*. The silence that followed was broken only by the long diminishing shriek of the dog.

"Guaranteed sixty-foot-diameter kill zone," the man who was on his way from Angola to Tulsa had said then.

Here was the second thing she already knew: this June 26 shipment was not the first such shipment her father had arranged. He had been arranging such shipments all through the spring and into the summer of 1984, a minimum of two and usually three or four a month, C-123s, Convair 440s, L-100s, whatever they sent up to be filled, rusty big bellies sitting on the back runways at Lauderdale–Hollywood and West

Palm and Opa-Locka and MIA waiting to be loaded with AK-47s, M-16s, MAC-10s, C-4, whatever was on the street, whatever was out there, whatever Dick McMahon could still promote on the strength of his connections, his contacts, his fifty years of doing a little business in Miami and in Houston and in Las Vegas and in Phoenix and in the piney woods of Alabama and Georgia.

These had not been easy shipments to assemble.

He had put these shipments together on credit, on goodwill, on a shared drink here and a promise there and a tale told at the Miami Springs Holiday Inn at two in the morning, on the shared yearning among what he called "these fellows I know for a long time" for one last score.

He had called in all his markers.

He had put himself on the line, spread paper all over the Southeast, thrown the dice just this one last time, one last bet on the million-dollar payday.

The million-dollar payday that was due to come with the delivery of the June 26 shipment.

The million-dollar payday that was scheduled to occur on the runway in Costa Rica where the June 26 shipment had just been unloaded.

One million American in Citibank traveler's checks, good as gold.

Of course I have to turn around half to these fellows I know a long time who advanced me the stuff.

Which complicates the position I'm in now.

Ellie. You see the position I'm in.

Five, ten years ago I might never have gotten out on a limb this way, I paid up front and got paid up front, did it clean, that was my strict motto, do it clean, cash and carry, maybe I'm getting old, maybe I played this

wrong, but hell, Ellie, think about it, when was I go-
ing to see another shot like this one.

Don't give me goddamn hindsight.

Hindsight is for shoe clerks.

Five, ten years ago, sure, I might have done it an-
other way, but five, ten years ago we weren't in the
middle of the goddamnest hot market anybody ever
saw. So what can you do. Strike while the iron is hot,
so you run a little risk, so you get out on a limb for a
change, it's all you can do as I figure it.

So anyway.

So what.

You can see I need this deal.

You can see I'm in a position where I need to go
down there and make the collection.

It was the figure that broke her heart.

The evenness of the figure.

The size of the figure.

The figure that was part of what she believed to be
a delusion, the figure that had been the *bel canto* of
her childhood, the figure that was now a memory, an
echo, a dream, a romance, an old man's fairy tale.

The million-dollar score, the million-dollar pop, the
million-dollar payday.

The pop that was already half owed to other people,
the payday that was already garnisheed.

The score that was not even a score anymore.

I'm in for a unit, my father's doing two, Wynn Jan-
klow would say to indicate investments of one and
two hundred million dollars.

Million-dollar score, million-dollar payday.

She had gone her own way.

She had made her own life.

She had married a man who did not count money in millions but in units.

She had turned a deaf ear, she had turned her back.

It might be you'd just called from wherever.

In the creased snapshot she had taken from her mother's bedroom her father was holding a bottle of beer and her mother was wearing a barbecue apron printed with pitchforks and the words OUT OF THE FRYING PAN INTO THE FIRE.

Or it might be that you hadn't.

She remembered the day the snapshot was taken.

Fourth of July, she was nine or ten, a friend of her father's had brought fireworks up from the border, fat little sizzler rockets she had not liked and sparklers that made fireflies in the hot desert twilight.

Half a margarita and I'm already flying, her mother had kept saying.

This is all right, her father had kept saying. Who needs the goombahs, we got our own show right here.

We had a life and now we don't and just because I'm your daughter I'm supposed to like it and I don't.

What's going to happen now, her father had said on the day she brought him home to the house in Sweetwater. Goddamn. Ellie. What's going to happen now.

I'll take care of it, she had said.

By eight o'clock on the morning of July 2 she had already checked out of the Hotel Colonial and was in the taxi on her way to the San José airport. By eight o'clock on the morning of July 2 she did not yet know that her father's obituary had appeared in that morning's Miami *Herald*, but she did know something else.

This was the third thing she already knew.

She had asked for her passport when she checked out.

Her own passport.

The passport she had left at the desk the night she arrived.

For the authorities, for safekeeping.

The clerk was quite certain that it had been returned to her.

Por cierto, he had repeated. *Certísimo.*

The airport taxi had been waiting outside.

If you would look again, she had said. An American passport. McMahon. Elena McMahon.

The clerk had opened the safe, removed several passports, fanned them on the desk, and shrugged.

None of the passports were American.

In the mailboxes behind the clerk she could see room keys, a few messages.

The box for her room was empty.

She considered this.

The clerk raised an index finger, tapped his temple, and smiled. *Tengo la solución,* he said. Since the passport had certainly been returned to her, the passport would doubtless be found in her room. Perhaps she would be so kind as to leave an address.

I don't think so, she had said, and walked to the open door.

Buen viaje, Señora Meyer, the clerk had called as she was getting into the airport taxi.

8

When she landed on the island at one-thirty on the afternoon of July 2 the sky was dark with clouds and the runway already swamped with the rain that would fall intermittently for the next week. The Costa Rican pilot had mentioned this possibility. "A few bands of showers that will never dampen the spirit of any vacationer," was how the pilot had put it in his English-language update from the front cabin. It had occurred to Elena as she sheltered the unfamiliar passport under her T-shirt and made a run for the terminal that these bands of showers would not in fact dampen the spirit of any vacationer, since there did not seem to be any vacationer in sight.

No golf bag, no tennis racket, no sunburned child in tow.

No anxious traveler with four overstuffed tote bags and one boarding pass for the six-seater hop to the more desirable island.

There did not even seem to be any airport employee in sight.

Only the half-dozen young men, wearing the short-sleeved uniforms of what seemed to be some kind of local military police, lounging just inside the closed glass doors to the terminal.

She had stopped, rain streaming down her face, waiting for the doors to slide open automatically.

When the doors did not open she had knocked on the glass.

After what seemed a considerable length of time, once she had been joined outside the glass door by the crew from her flight, one of the men inside had detached himself from the others and inserted a key to open the door.

Thank you, she had said.

Move on, he had said.

She had moved on.

Gate after gate was unlit. The moving sidewalks were not moving, the baggage carousels were silent. Metal grilles had been lowered over the doors to the coffee bars and concessions, even the shop that promised OPEN 24 HOURS DUTY-FREE. She had steeled herself on the plane to make direct eye contact when she went through immigration but the lone immigration official had examined the passport without interest, stamped it, and handed it back to her, never meeting her eyes.

"Where you stay," he had said, pen poised to complete whatever form required this information.

She had tried to think of a plausible answer.

"You mean while I'm here," she had said, stalling. "You mean what hotel."

"Correct, correct, what hotel." He was bored, impatient. "Ramada, Royal Caribe, Intercon, what."

"Ramada," she had said.

She had gotten a taxi for the Ramada and then, once the doors were closed, told the driver that she had changed her mind and wanted to go to the Intercon. She had registered at the Intercon as Elise Meyer. As soon as she got upstairs she called Barry Sedlow's beeper and left the number of the hotel.

Twenty minutes later the telephone had rung.

She had picked it up but said nothing.

So far so good, Barry Sedlow said. You're where you should be.

She thought about this.

She had left the number of the hotel on his beeper but she had not left the number of her room.

To get through to the room he had to know how she was registered.

Had to know that the passport was in the name Elise Meyer.

She said nothing.

Just sit tight, he said. Someone's going to be in touch.

Still she said nothing.

Losing radio contact, he said. Hel-lo-oh.

There had been a silence.

Okay I get it, he had said finally. You don't want to talk, don't talk. But do yourself a favor? Relax. Go down to the pool, tip the boy to set up a chaise, get some sun, order one of those drinks with the cherries and the pineapple and the little umbrellas, you're there as a tourist, try acting like one, just tell the operator to switch your calls, don't worry about their finding you, they're going to find you all right.

She had done this. She had not spoken to Barry Sedlow but she had done what he said to do.

I do not know why (another instance of *what "changed" her, what "motivated" her, what made her do it*) but she had put down the telephone and waited for a break in the rain and then done exactly what Barry Sedlow said to do.

At four that afternoon and again at noon the next day and again at noon of the day after that, she had bought the local paper and whatever day-old American papers she could find in the coffee shop and gone down to the Intercon pool and tipped the boy to set up a chaise within range of the pool shack telephone. She had sat on the chaise under the gray sky and she had read the newspapers all the way through, one by one, beginning with the local paper and progressing to whatever Miami *Herald* or New York *Times* or *USA Today* had come in that morning. She read on the chaise at the Intercon pool about the dock strike in the Grenadines. She read on the chaise at the Intercon pool about the demonstration in Pointe-à-Pitre to protest the arrest of the leader of the independence movement. She read in a week-old *USA Today* about the effect of fish oil on infertile pandas in distant zoos. The only stories she avoided outright, there on the chaise at the Intercon pool, were those having to do with the campaign. She moved past any story having to do with the campaign. She preferred stories having to do with natural forces, stories about new evidence of reef erosion in the Maldives, say, or recently released research on the deep cold Pacific welling of El Niño.

About unusual movements of wind charted off the coast of Africa.

About controversial data predicting the probability of earthquakes measuring over 5.5 Richter.

American, the pool boy had said when she tipped him the first day with an American dollar. Whole lot of Americans coming in.

Really, she had said, by way of closing the conversation.

Good for business, he had said, by way of reopening it.

She had looked around the empty pool, the unused chaises stacked against the shack. I guess they don't swim much, she had said.

He had giggled and slapped his thigh with a towel. Do not swim much, he said finally. No.

By the third day she had herself begun noticing the Americans. Several in the coffee shop the night before, all men. Several more in the lobby, laughing together as they stood at the entrance waiting to get into an unmarked armored van.

The van had CD plates.

Swear to Christ, that deal in Chalatenango, I did something like three and a half full clips, one of the Americans had said.

Shit, another had said. You know the difference between one of them and a vampire? You drive a stake through a vampire's heart, the fucker dies.

No Americans at the pool.

Until now.

She had become aware as she was reading the local paper that one of the men she had seen waiting to get into the van with the CD plates was standing between her chaise and the pool, blocking the tiled walkway, smoking a cigarette as he surveyed the otherwise empty pool area.

His back was to her.

His warm-up jacket was lettered 25TH DIVISION TROPIC LIGHTNING.

She realized that she was reading for the third time the same follow-up on a rash of thefts and carjackings in the immediate vicinity of Cyril E. King International Airport on St. Thomas.

Excuse me, she said. Do you know what time it is.

He flicked his cigarette in the direction of the clock over the pool shack counter.

The clock read 1:10.

She put down the local paper and picked up the Miami *Herald*.

She continued reading the Miami *Herald* until she reached page sixteen of the B section.

Page sixteen of the B section of the July 2 Miami *Herald*, two days late.

McMAHON, Richard Allen: age 74, died under care of physician June 30, 1984, at Clearview Convalescent Lodge, South Kendall. No services are scheduled.

She folded the newspaper, got up from the chaise and edged her way past the American in the warm-up jacket.

Pardon me, he said. Ma'am.

Excuse me, she said.

Outside the hotel she got a taxi and told the driver to take her to the American embassy. The "little business" (as she thought of it) at the main embassy gate took ten minutes. The "kind of spooky coincidence" (as she thought of it) or "incident" (as it immediately became known) at the embassy picnic took another ten minutes. When she got back to her room at the Intercon at approximately two-thirty on the afternoon of July 4 she wrote two letters, one to Catherine and one to Wynn Janklow, which she took to an air express office to be shipped for delivery the next day in the United States. *Sweet bird,* the letter to Catherine began. She had spoken to Catherine twice from San José and again the evening she arrived on the island but the calls had been unsatisfactory and now she could not reach her.

> *Tried to call you a few minutes ago but you had signed out to go to Cape Ann with Francie and her parents—didn't know how to reach you and there are two things I need you to know right away. The first thing I need you to know is that I'm asking your father to pick you up and bring you to Malibu for a while. Just until I get back from this trip. You don't need summer credits anyway and he can probably arrange a way you can do the S.A.T. prep out there. The second thing I need you to know is I love you. Sometimes we argue about things but I think we both know I only argue because I want your life to be happy and good. Want you not to waste your time. Not to waste your talents. Not to let who you are get mixed up with anybody else's idea of who you should be.*
>
> *I love you the most. XXXXXXXX, M.*
>
> *P.S. If anyone else comes and wants to take you from school for any reason repeat ANY REASON do not repeat DO NOT go with him or her.*

The letter to Wynn Janklow was short, because she had reached him, at the house in Malibu, as soon as she got back from the embassy. She had placed the call from a pay phone in the Intercon lobby. Had he not answered the phone she would have waited in the lobby until he did, because she needed to talk to Wynn before chancing any situation (the elevator, say, or the corridor upstairs) in which she might be alone.

Any situation in which something might happen to prevent her from telling Wynn what it was she wanted him to do.

Wynn had answered the phone.

Wynn had told her that he had just walked in off a flight from Taipei.

She had told Wynn what it was she wanted him to do.

She had not mentioned the kind of spooky coincidence at the embassy picnic.

My understanding is that Dick McMahon will not be a problem, she had heard the familiar but unplaceable voice say at the embassy picnic.

The steel band that was playing Sousa marches had momentarily fallen silent and the familiar but unplaceable voice had carried across the tent.

Deek McMaa-aan was the way the familiar voice pronounced the name. *My understanding is that Deek McMaa-aan will not be a problem.*

She had not placed the voice until she saw the Salvadoran across the tent.

Here is my concern, she remembered the Salvadoran saying in the Pan Am lounge at the Miami airport as he fingered the envelope Barry Sedlow had slipped him. *We have a little problem here.*

Transit passenger, she remembered Barry Sedlow saying in the car just after he shot out the streetlight

with the 9mm Browning. *Already on the six-thirty
back to San Sal. Not our deal.*

The Salvadoran was the kind of spooky coincidence.

The Salvadoran was why she called Wynn.

The Salvadoran was why she tried to call Catherine.

The Salvadoran was why she wrote the letters and
took them to the air express office for next-day delivery to Catherine and to Wynn.

The Salvadoran was why she went from the air express office to a local office of the Bank of America,
where she obtained eleven thousand dollars in cash,
the sum of the cash available on Elena McMahon's
various credit cards.

The Salvadoran was why she then destroyed
the cards.

*My understanding is that Dick McMahon will not
be a problem.*

Not our deal, Barry Sedlow had said, but it was.

She wrote the letters and she arranged for Wynn to
take care of Catherine and she got the eleven thousand
dollars in cash and she destroyed the credit cards
because she had no way of knowing what kind of
problem Dick McMahon's daughter might be seen
to be.

Half a generation after the fact, from where I sit at my
desk in an apartment on the upper east side of Man-
hattan, it would be easy to conclude that Elena's actions that afternoon did not entirely make sense, easy
to assume that at some point in the hour between
learning her father was dead and seeing the Salvadoran she had cracked, panicked, gone feral, a trapped

animal trying to hide her young and stay alert in the wild, awake in the ether, alive on the ground.

All I can tell you is what she did.

All I can tell you is that at that time in that place there was a logic to what she did.

Wynn, the second of the two letters she wrote that afternoon read.

What I couldn't tell you on the phone was that something bad is happening. I don't know what it is. So please please do this one thing for me.

P.S., the postscript read.

You have to pick her up yourself. I mean don't send Rudich.

Rudich was someone who had worked for Wynn's father and now worked for Wynn. Rudich was who did things for Wynn. Rudich had a first name but no one ever used it and she had forgotten it. Rudich was who Wynn would call if he needed somebody to fly to Wyoming to take a ranch out of escrow. Rudich was who Wynn would send if he needed somebody to deliver a contract in person the next morning in Tokyo. Rudich was probably who now called the caterer to lay on the tennis lunches.

Rudich could do anything but Rudich could not do this one thing she needed done.

Please please do this.

Love. Still. E.

9

The last time I was in Los Angeles I made a point of going to see Wynn Janklow.

"Why not come by the house Sunday," he had said on the telephone. "I'm having some people, we'll talk, bring a racket."

I made an excuse to go instead to his office in Century City.

I admired, at his prompting, the photographs taken a few months before at Catherine's wedding.

"Big blowout," he said. "Under the *huppah* on the beach at sunset, I flew Bobby Short out to play during dinner, then two bands and fireworks, I'm still finding champagne glasses in the shrubbery but what the hell, great kids, both of them."

I appreciated, again at his prompting, the view of Catalina from his office windows, the clarity of the atmosphere in spite of what he referred to as "all this enviro-freak sky-is-falling shit which as God is my witness I hear even from people I call my friends."

I waited until the secretary had brought in the requisite silver tray with the requisite folded linen napkin, the requisite two bottles of Evian, the requisite Baccarat tumblers.

Only when the secretary had left the room and closed the door did I ask Wynn Janklow to try to remember what he had thought when he received first the call and one day later this letter from Elena.

He had furrowed his brow for my benefit. "That would have been, let me think, when."

Nineteen eighty-four, I said. July 1984.

Wynn Janklow swiveled his chair and gazed out the window, squinting, as if 1984 might materialize just off Catalina.

No big deal, he said then. As he remembered he had to be in New York that week anyway, he flew into Logan instead, got a car to take him down to Newport, he and Catherine had been in New York by midnight.

Big killer heat wave, he remembered.

You know the kind.

The kind where you step out of the car onto the street and you sink into the asphalt and if you don't move fast you're methane.

He remembered he had Catherine call Elena that night, report she was scarfing Maine lobster in the Hollywood Suite at the Regency.

Great kid even then. Always a great kid.

True enough, on the money, now that I mentioned it there had been some trick about calling Elena, the hotel didn't have her registered right, you had to ask for somebody else, she had given him the name when she called and he had given the name to Catherine.

Elise Meyer, I said.

Elise Meyer, he repeated. No problem, he was glad to be able to do what Elena wanted.

He had been here and Elena had been there but no problem, they stayed on good terms, they had this great kid after all, plus they were adults, unlike some people who got separated or divorced or whatever he and Elena had always maintained a very civilized kind of relationship.

True enough, again on the money, her call had seemed maybe a little overwrought.

Fourth of July, he was just off the plane from Taipei, thinking he'd play a little tennis, work off the jet lag before he had to be in New York.

And then this call from Elena.

Whoa, hold on, he remembered saying. So something happened at the embassy, some clerk gave you the runaround, let me make a few calls, shoot a rocket up the fucker's fat ass.

You don't understand, he remembered Elena saying.

You have to be here to understand, he remembered Elena saying.

Wynn Janklow had again gazed out the window. "End of sad story," he said.

There had been a silence.

"The sad story is what," I said finally. "You think Elena might have been right? Is that the sad story?" I tried for a neutral tone, a therapist guiding the client back. I wanted to see him confront that hour during which Elena had gone feral. "You think maybe you did have to be there to understand?"

He did not at first respond.

"Maybe you noticed this gadget I have on the wall there," he said then.

He got up and walked to an electronic Mercator projection mounted on the wall, one of those devices on which it is possible to read the time anywhere in the world by watching part of the map pass into darkness as another part emerges into daylight.

"You can watch the sun rise and set anyplace you want," he said. "Right here. Standing right here looking at this." He jabbed at the map with an index finger. "But it doesn't tell you shit about what's happening there."

He sat down behind his desk.

He picked up a paperweight, then buzzed an intercom.

"It's just a toy," he said then. "Frankly it's just something I use when I'm making calls, I look over there and I can see at a glance who's likely to be awake. Meaning I can call them."

He had again buzzed the intercom.

"And in all fairness, I have to admit, sometimes they're awake and sometimes they aren't." He had looked up with relief as the secretary opened the door. "If you could locate a few stamps for her parking ticket, Raina, I'll walk our guest downstairs."

10

Of course Elena might have been right.

Of course you had to be there to understand.

Of course, had you not been there, it might have seemed a definite stretch to call what happened at the embassy Fourth of July picnic an "incident."

Of course, had you not been there, what happened at the embassy Fourth of July picnic might have suggested not an "incident" but merely that it was time to make a few calls, shoot a few rockets up a few fat asses.

"The incident" was what Alex Brokaw called it when he suggested to his DCM that it might be useful to run a background on Elise Meyer. "I'll have to excuse myself to follow up on a little incident," was what the DCM said by way of cutting short a conversation with the Brown & Root project manager who had just arrived to supervise the hardening of the perimeter around the residence. "Just crossing the t's and dotting the i's on a rather troubling incident we had here," was what the DCM said when he put through the request for the background on Elise Meyer.

This was the rather troubling incident in its entirety:

"I'm an American citizen and I need to speak to a consular officer," Elena McMahon had said when she walked into the tented area reserved for the embassy picnic.

The traditional Fourth of July picnic held by every American embassy and open to any American citizen who happens to be in the vicinity.

The Fourth of July embassy picnic that must have seemed, given a country in which any American citizen who happened to be in the vicinity happened also to be in the official or covert employ of one or another branch of the embassy, a trying tradition at best.

She needed, she had said, to replace a lost passport.

She did not want to interrupt the picnic, she had said, but she had gone to the consulate and the guard at the gate said the consulate was closed for the holiday, and she needed her passport replaced immediately.

She needed her passport replaced immediately because she needed to return to the United States immediately.

The woman had seemed, according to the consular officer who was finally located to deal with her, "a little confused," and "unable or unwilling" to accept his "offer to try to clear up the confusion."

The confusion of course was that this woman already had her passport.

Her presence inside the tented area was proof that she already had her passport.

The confusion with this woman had begun at the gate.

She had also told the marine on duty at the gate that she had lost her passport, and when he told her to re-

turn the next morning when the consular office re-
opened she had insisted that tomorrow would be too
late, she needed to see a consular officer now.

The marine had explained that this would be impossible because all the consular officers were at the
Fourth of July picnic.

The Fourth of July picnic that unfortunately she
could not attend because guests were required to present an American passport.

At which point this woman had produced her
passport.

And left it, as any other guest not known to the embassy would have left his or her passport, with the
guard at the entrance to the tented area.

This woman had left her passport and signed the
embassy guest book.

There it was, he could show it to her, her signature:
Elise Meyer.

Here it was, the guard could and would return it to
her, her passport: *Elise Meyer.*

That was the confusion.

According to the consular officer she had taken the
passport and held it out, as if she were about to show
or give it to him. There had been a moment of silence
before she spoke. "This was just to get me in because I
need to explain something," she had said, and then
she had fallen silent.

She had been looking across the tent.

The steel band had stopped playing.

The woman had seemed, the consular officer reported, "very interested in some of our Salvadoran
friends."

"Neat idea, by the way, the steel band," the consular officer had added, "but next year it might be

appropriate to tell them, 'Rule Britannia' isn't ours."

It was at the point when the steel band struck up "Rule Britannia" that the woman had put the passport in her bag, closed the bag, and walked out of the tent and across the lawn and out the gate.

"You were about to explain something," the consular officer had said as she started to walk away.

"Forget it," she had said without turning back.

That was the reason for ordering the background.

The background that was ordered to get a line on who she was and what she was doing there.

The background that threw up the glitch.

The background that turned up flat.

No history.

The passport bearing the name Elise Meyer showed that it had been issued on June 30 1984 at the United States Passport Agency in Miami, but the United States Passport Agency in Miami reported no record of having issued a passport in the name Elise Meyer.

That was the glitch.

II

The young FBI agent who had flown down from the Miami office had opened the initial interview by mentioning the glitch.

She had looked puzzled.

The discrepancy, the anomaly, whatever she wanted to call it.

He was certain that she could clear this immediately.

He was sure that she would have a simple explanation for the glitch.

The anomaly.

The discrepancy.

She had offered no explanation at all.

She had merely shrugged. "At my age I don't actually find discrepancies too surprising," she had said. "You must be what? Twenty-six, twenty-seven?"

He was twenty-five.

He had decided to try another tack.

"Assuming for the moment that someone provided you with apparently inauthentic documentation," he began.

"*You're* assuming that," she said. "Naturally. Because you haven't had a whole lot of experience with the way things work. You still think things work the way they're supposed to work. *I'm* assuming something more along the lines of business as usual."

"Excuse me?"

"I guess you must work in an office where nobody ever makes a mistake," she said. "I guess where you work nobody ever hits the wrong key because they're in a rush to go on break."

"I don't see your point."

"You don't think it's possible that some low-level GS-whatever in the passport office accidentally deleted my record?"

This was in fact a distinct possibility, but he chose to ignore it. "Apparently inauthentic documentation is sometimes provided for the purpose of placing the carrier in a position where they can be blackmailed into doing something they wouldn't otherwise do."

"Is that something you learned at Quantico?"

He ignored this. "In other words," he repeated, "someone could have placed you in such a position." He paused for emphasis. "Someone could be using you."

"For what," she said.

"If there were a plot," the agent said.

"That's your invention. This whole plot business. Your movie. Not anybody else's."

The agent paused. She had agreed to the interview. She had not been uncooperative. Because she had not been uncooperative he let this pass, but what she had said was not entirely accurate. The plot to assassinate Alex Brokaw was not his invention at all. There were various theories around the embassy and also in Miami about whose invention it was, the most popular of which was that Alex Brokaw himself had engineered the report in an effort to derail a certain two-track approach then favored at State, but the existence of a plot, once it was mentioned by what the cable traffic called "a previously reliable source," had to be accepted at face value. Documentable steps had to be taken. The record at State had to duly show the formation of a crisis management team on the Caribbean desk. The paperwork had to duly show that wall maps had been requisitioned, with colored pins to indicate known players. The concertina perimeter around the embassy overflow office structures had to be duly reinforced. On the record. All AM/EMBASSY dependents and nonessential personnel had to be duly encouraged to take home leave. In triplicate. All American citizens with access to AM/EMBASSY personnel and uncleared backgrounds had to be interviewed.

Duly.

Including this one.

This one had access to AM/EMBASSY personnel by virtue of being on the island.

This one had thrown a glitch.

Something about this one's use of the phrase "your movie" bothered him but he let that go too.

"If there were a plot," he repeated, "someone could be using you."

"Those are your words."

In the silence that followed the young man had clicked his ballpoint pen on the table. There were other things about this one that bothered him, but it was important to keep what bothered him out of this picture. It was possible they might be experiencing a syntactical problem, a misunderstanding that could be cleared up by restatement. "Why not put it in your own words," he said finally.

She fished a loose cigarette from her pocket and then, when he made the error of interpreting this as an encouraging sign, replaced the cigarette in her pocket, ignoring the match he was still fumbling to strike.

"There could be a game in there somewhere," she had said then. "And I could be in there somewhere."

"In the plot."

"In the game."

The agent said nothing.

"In whatever you want to call it," she said then. "It's your movie."

"Let's approach this from another angle," he said after a silence. "You came here from San José. Costa Rica. Yet no record exists showing you ever entered Costa Rica. So let's start there."

"You want to know how I got into Costa Rica." Her voice had again suggested cooperation.

"Exactly."

"You don't even need a passport to enter Costa Rica. An American citizen can enter Costa Rica on a tourist card. From a travel agency."

"But you didn't."

There had been another silence.

"I'm going to say something," she said then. "You're going to get it or you won't. I haven't been here long, but I've been here long enough to notice a lot of Americans here. I notice them on the street, I notice them at the hotel, I notice them all over. I don't know if they have their own passports. I don't know whose passports they have. I don't know whose passport I have. All I know is, they aren't on vacation."

Again she took the loose cigarette from her pocket and again she put it back.

"So I'd suggest you just think for a while about

what they're doing here," she had said then. "And I bet you could pretty much figure how I got into Costa Rica."

Subject "Elise Meyer" acknowledges entering country in possession of apparently inauthentic documentation but provides no further information concerning either the source of said documentation or her purpose in entering said country, the agent's preliminary report read. *Recommendation: continued surveillance and investigation until such time as identity of subject can be verified, as well as subject's purpose in entering said country.*

This initial interview took place on July 10 1984.

A second interview, during which subject and interrogator reiterated their respective points, took place on July 11 1984.

Elena McMahon moved from the Intercon to the Surfrider on July 12.

It was August 14 when Treat Morrison flew down from Washington on the American that landed at ten a.m. and, when he stopped by the Intercon to leave his bag, happened to see her sitting by herself in the Intercon coffee shop.

Sitting by herself at the round table set for eight.

Wearing the white dress.

Eating the chocolate parfait and bacon.

When he got to the embassy later that day he learned from Alex Brokaw's DCM that the woman he had seen in the Intercon coffee shop had arrived on the island on July 2 on an apparently falsified American passport issued in the name Elise Meyer. At his request the DCM had arranged to have him briefed on

the progress of the continuing FBI investigation meant
to ascertain who Elise Meyer was and what she was
doing there. Later it occurred to him that there would
have been at that time in that embassy certain people
who already knew who Elise Meyer was and what she
was doing there, but it did not occur to him then.

Three

I should understand Treat Morrison.
I studied him, I worked him up.

I researched him, I interviewed him, I listened to him, watched him.

I came to recognize his way of speaking, came to know how to read the withheld phrasing, the fast dying fall or diminuendo that would render key words barely audible, the sudden rise and overemphasis on the insignificant part of the sentence (". . . and by the *way*"), the rush or explosion of syllables jammed together (". . . and the hell it *is* . . ."), the raising of the entirely rhetorical question (". . . and . . . *should* I have regrets?"), the thoughtful acting out of the entirely rhetorical answer (head tilted up, a gaze into the middle distance, then "I . . . don't think . . . *so*"), the unconvincingly brisk reiteration: ". . . and I have *no* regrets."

No regrets.

Treat Morrison had no regrets.

Quite early in the course of these dealings with Treat Morrison I came to regard him as fundamentally dishonest. Not dishonest in the sense that he "lied," or deliberately misrepresented events as he himself construed them (he did not, he never did, he was scrupulous to a fault about reporting exactly what he believed to be true), but dishonest in the more radical sense, dishonest in that he remained incapable of seeing the thing straight. At the outset I viewed this as an idiosyncrasy or a defect of character, in either case singular, peculiar to the individual, a personal eccentricity. I came only later to see that what I viewed as personal was deep in the grain of who he was and where he came from.

Let me give you a paragraph from my notes.

Not interview notes, not raw notes, but early draft notes, notes lacking words and clauses and marked with *CH* for "check" and *TK* for "to come," meaning I didn't have it then but planned to get it, notes worked up in the attempt to get something on paper that might open a way to a lead:

> *Treat Austin Morrison was born in San Francisco at a time, 1930, when San Francisco was still remote, isolated, separated physically from the rest of the United States by the ranges of mountains that closed off when the heavy snows came, separated emotionally by the implacable presence of the Pacific, by the ???TK and by the ???TK and by the fogs that blew in from the Farallons every afternoon at four or five. His father held a minor city sinecure, jury commissioner in the municipal court*

There this particular note toward a lead skids to an abrupt stop. Scratched in pencil after the typed words "municipal court" is a comma, then one further penciled clause:

> *a job he owed to his wife's well-placed relatives in*
> *the Irish wards (??CH "wards") south of Market*
> *Street.*

More false starts:

> *The son of a parochial school teacher and a minor*
> *city official in San Francisco, Treat Austin Morri*
> *son enrolled at the University of California at*
> *Berkeley when it was still offering a free college*
> *education to any qualified California high school*
> *graduate who could scrape up the $27.50 (??CH)*
> *registration fee plus whatever little he or she could*
> *live on. The man who would later become Amer*
> *ica's man-on-the-spot in the world's hottest spots,*
> *ambassador-at-large with a top-secret portfolio,*
> *earned part of his college costs by parking cars at*
> *the elite Hotel Claremont in Oakland, the rest by*

> *Treat Austin Morrison may have been Saturday's*
> *hero on the football field (XXX BETTER LINE*
> *TK), the University of California's own All-PAC*
> *8 (??CH) quarterback, but Saturday night would*
> *find him back in the kitchen at the exclusive Phi*
> *Gamma Delta house, where he paid for his room*
> *and board by hashing, washing dishes and wait*
> *ing table for the affluent party animals who called*
> *themselves his fraternity brothers and from whom*
> *he borrowed the textbooks he could not afford to*
> *buy. The discipline developed in those years*
> *stands him in good stead as*

T.A.M. was raised an only child

T.A.M., the only son and during most of his formative years the only living child of a

T.A.M., the only son and after his older sister's suicide the only living child

There are pages of such draft notes, a thick sheaf of them, most of them uncharacteristically (for me) focused on the subject's early deprivations and childhood pluck (uncharacteristically for me because it has not been my actual experience that the child is father to the man), all of them aborted. I see now that there was a clear common thread in these failed starts, that I was trying to deal with something about Treat Morrison that continued to elude me: this was a man who was at the time I interviewed him living and working at the heart of the American political establishment. This was a man who could pick up the telephone and affect the Dow, reach the foreign minister of any one of a dozen NATO countries, the Oval Office itself. This was a man generally perceived as a mover, a shaker, a can-do guy, someone who appeared to thrive on negotiation, on dealing, on calculation and calibration and adjustment, the very stuff that defines a successful social operator. Yet this remained someone who projected nothing so much as an extreme, even resistant loneliness, an isolation so impenetrable as to seem to demand analysis, examination, a reason why.

Treat Morrison himself appeared to have no interest in examining what I am distressed to notice I was choosing to call "his formative years."

I would not hear from him about early deprivations or childhood pluck, nor would I get from him even the slightest clue that the traditional actors in the family drama (or, in the vocabulary into which I appear to have been sinking, the formative dynamic) had been in his case other than casual acquaintances.

"As far as I know she was regarded as an excellent teacher," he said about his mother. "Very well thought of, very esteemed by the sisters who ran the school." He paused, as if weighing this for fairness. "Of course she was a Catholic," he said then.

Since this afterthought was the most specific and least remote information he had so far seemed inclined to convey, I decided to pursue it. "Then you were raised a Catholic," I began, tentatively, expecting, if not revelation, at least confirmation or correction.

What I got was zero.

What I got was Treat Morrison waiting, at bay, his fingers tented.

"Or were you," I said.

He said nothing.

"Raised a Catholic," I said.

He aligned a square crystal paperweight with the edge of his desk blotter.

"Not to say that I entirely disagreed with many of the pertinent precepts," he said then, "but as far as the whole religious business went, it just wasn't an area that particularly interested me."

"He was very well liked around the courthouse," he said about his father. "As far as I know."

"It was something that happened," he said about the death of his sister at age nineteen. "I was twelve, thirteen years old when it happened, there were the seven years between us, seven years at that age could be a lifetime, to all intents and purposes Mary Katherine was someone I barely knew."

"For all anyone knows it was an accident," he said when I tried to follow up on this subject. "She was watching the seals, the surf came up and took her, Mary Katherine never had any coordination, she was always in the emergency room, if she wasn't breaking her ankle she was dropping a bicycle on her leg or knocking herself out with a tetherball or every other damn thing."

"I guess I didn't see any useful reason to dwell on that," he said when I suggested that very few people who get accidentally taken by the surf while watching the seals happen to have mailed goodbye notes to (although not to their mother or father or brother) three former teachers at Lowell High School and a former boyfriend who had recently left to go through OCS at Fort Lewis. MISSION TEEN A HOMEFRONT CASUALTY, the headline read in the San Francisco *Chronicle* the morning after the letters began to surface. I had found it on microfiche. LOWELL GRAD WROTE FINAL DEAR JOHN. "There you see the goddamn media again," Treat Morrison said about this. "Goddamn media was meddling even then in something they couldn't possibly begin to understand."

"Which would have been what." I recall trying for an offhand delivery. "What was it exactly that the media didn't begin to understand."

Treat Morrison said nothing for a moment. "A lot of people get some big mystical kick out of chewing over things that happened forty, forty-five years ago," he said then. "Little sad stories about being misunderstood by their mother or getting snubbed at school or whatever. I'm not saying there's anything wrong with this, I'm not saying it's self-indulgent or self-pitying or any other damn thing. I'm just saying I can't afford it. So I don't do it."

I find in my notes and taped interviews only two instances in which Treat Morrison volunteered anything about his background that could be construed as personal. The first such instance is buried deep in a taped discussion of what a two-state solution would mean to Israel. Three-quarters of the way through a sixty-minute tape, at 44:19 to be exact, Treat Morrison falls silent. When he resumes talking it is not about two-state versus one-state for Israel but about having once had some pictures framed for his mother. It seemed that his mother had broken a hip and been forced to move from her house in the Mission district to a Mercy convalescent home in Woodside. It seemed that he had stopped to see her on his way to a meeting in Saigon. It seemed that she had kept mentioning these pictures, snapshots of him and his sister at a place they used to go on the Russian River. "She'd had them stuck in a mirror, she wanted them at the new place, I thought I'd get them put in a frame, you know those frames that take four or five little pictures. So fine. But when I go to pick it up, the clerk has written on the package *'kids playing by stream.'*"

47:17. A pause on the tape.

"So that was a lesson," he says then.

Actually I knew immediately what the lesson would have been.

I had been working this row long enough to make the inductive leaps required by Treat Morrison's rather cryptic staccato.

The lesson would have been that no one else will ever view our lives exactly as we do: someone else had looked at the snapshots and seen the two children but had failed to hear the music, had failed even to know or care that he or she was lacking the emotional score. Just as someone else could have looked at the snapshot Elena McMahon took from her mother's bedroom and seen her father holding the beer and her mother in the apron printed with pitchforks ("*man and woman at barbecue*") but never seen the fat little sizzler rockets, never seen the sparklers that made fireflies in the hot desert twilight. Never heard *half a margarita and I'm already flying*, never heard *who needs the goombahs, we got our own show right here*.

I knew all that.

The conventions of the interview nonetheless required that I ask the obvious question, follow up, encourage the subject to keep talking.

50:05. "What was the lesson," I hear myself say on the tape.

"In the first place," Treat Morrison says on the tape, "it wasn't some 'stream,' we didn't have 'streams' in California, 'streams' are what they have in England, or Vermont, it was the goddamn Russian River."

Another pause.

"In the second place we weren't 'playing.' She was eleven, for Christ's sake, I was four, what would we '*play*.' We were getting our picture taken, that's the only reason we were even together."

And then, without a beat: "Which has to kind of give you an insight into how differently an Israeli and a Palestinian might view the same little event or the same little piece of land."

That was one of Treat Morrison's two ventures into the personal.

The second such venture is also on tape, and also has to do with his mother. It seemed that he had arranged to have his mother driven to Berkeley to see him receive an honor of some sort. He did not remember what the honor had been. What the honor had been was not the point. The point was that because they would have no other time alone, he had made a reservation to take his mother to dinner at the Claremont Hotel.

"Big white gingerbread job, just as you start up into the hills," he says on the tape. "Funny thing was, I don't know if you knew this, I parked cars there as an undergraduate."

"I think I did know that." My voice on the tape.

"Well then. So." A pause, then a rush of words. "My memory of this place was of someplace very very—I mean the definition of glamour. I mean at that time for that side of the bay this place was pretty much the *ne plus ultra* of big-deal sophistication. So I take my mother there. And it still looked the same, same big lobby, same big wide corridors, except now it looked to me like a cruise ship beached in maybe 1943. I hadn't walked into the place in twenty-five years. I mean, hell, I graduated in 1951, and I swear to Christ they still have the same piano player in the lobby. Playing the same goddamn songs. 'Where or When.' 'Tenderly.' 'It Might as Well Be Spring.' Now the night I'm there with my mother it so happened it *was* spring, spring 1975 to be exact, April, goddamn Saigon closing down, and outside the hotel while my mother and I are having dinner there's this torchlight parade, march, conga line, whatever, all these kids carrying torches and chanting *Ho Ho / Ho Chi Minh.* Plus something about me personally, I frankly don't even remember what it was, that's not the point. And inside the piano player keeps pounding out 'It Might as Well Be Spring.' And I'm sitting there hoping my mother doesn't understand that the kids are outside because I'm inside. 'Mary Katherine died thirty-three years ago tomorrow,' my mother says. Real casual, you understand, never looks up from the menu. 'I believe I'll take the prime rib,' she says then. 'What will you take.' What I took was another goddamn double bourbon, bring two while you're at it."

Ho Ho / Ho Chi Minh

The war Mister Morrison / Will not win

Was what they chanted outside the Claremont that night.

Something else I found on microfiche.

The first time Treat Morrison was alone with Elena he mentioned Mary Katherine's death.

"Why did she do it," Elena said.

"I don't have an answer for that kind of tragedy," he said.

"Which kind do you have an answer for," Elena said.

Treat Morrison studied her for a moment. "I read you," he said then.

"I read you too," she said.

Of course she did, of course he did.

Of course they read each other.

Of course they knew each other, understood each other, recognized each other, took one look and got each other, had to be with each other, saw the color drain out of what they saw when they were not looking at each other.

They were the same person.

They were equally remote.

2

D REAM, the notebook entry is headed, all in caps.
The notebook, a spiral-bound Clairefontaine
with a red cover and pale-gray three-eighth-inch graph
paper inside, was one kept by Elena Janklow during
the months in 1981 and 1982 immediately before she
left the house on the Pacific Coast Highway and once
again became (at least for a while, at least provision-
ally) Elena McMahon.

"*I seem to have had an operation,*" Elena Janklow's
account of the dream begins. Her handwriting, all but
the last entries made in the same black fine-point pen.
"*Unspecified but unsuccessful. I am 'sewn back up
again,' but roughly, as after an autopsy. It is agreed (I
have agreed to this) that there is no point in doing a
careful job, I am to die, a few days hence. The day on
which I am assigned to die is a Sunday, Christmas
Day. Wynn and Catherine and I are in Wynn's father's apartment in New York, where the death will
take place, by gas. I am concerned about how the gas
will be cleared out of the apartment but no one else
seems to be.*

"*It occurs to me that I must shop for Saturday night*

dinner, and make it special, since this will be my last day alive. I go out on 57th Street and along Sixth Avenue, very crowded and cold, in a bundled-up robe. My feet are very loosely sewn and I am afraid the stitching (basting really) will come out, also that my face is not on straight (again as in an autopsy it has been peeled down and put back up), and getting sadder and sadder.

"As I shop it occurs to me that maybe I could live: why must I die? I mention this to Wynn. He says then call the doctor, call Arnie Stine in California and tell him. Ask Arnie if you need to die tomorrow. I call Arnie Stine in California and he says no, if that's what I want, of course I do not need to die tomorrow. He can 'arrange it for later' if I want. I continue shopping, for Christmas dinner now as well as for Saturday night. I get a capon to roast for Christmas. I am euphoric, relieved, but still concerned that I cannot be sewn back together properly. Arnie Stine says I can be but I am afraid I will fall apart while shopping, walking on my loose feet.

"I am trying to be careful when I wake up."

It was Catherine who found the spiral-bound notebook, the summer Wynn picked her up at school and brought her first to the Hollywood Suite at the Regency and then to the house on the Pacific Coast Highway. She had been looking through the desk in the pantry for takeout menus when she found the notebook, on which her mother had printed, in Magic Marker, the word MENUS. In fact there actually were menus in the notebook, not takeout menus of course but menus Elena had made up for dinners or lunches, a dozen or more of them, with notes on quantities and recipes ("*three lbs lamb for navarin serves eight outside*"), cropping up at random among the other entries.

The peculiarity was in the other entries. They were not exactly the kind of notes a professional writer or reporter might make, but neither were they conventional "diary" notes, the confessions or private thoughts set down by a civilian. What was peculiar about these entries was that they reflected elements of both modes, the personal and the reportorial, with no apparent distinction between the two. There were scraps of what appeared to be overheard dialogue, there were lists of roses and other garden plants. There were quotes from and comments on news stories, there were scraps of remembered poetry. There were what appear to have been passing thoughts, some random, some less so. And there were of course the dreams.

"I get a little spacey when I stop smoking, probably because I get too much oxygen."

"What he's best at getting hold of is other people's money."

This much I can see without going outside: climbing Cecile Brunner roses, Henri Martin roses, Paulii roses, Chicago Peace roses, Scarlet Fire roses, blue and white amaryllis, scabiosa, Meyer lemons, star jasmine, santolina, butterfly bush, yarrow, blue lavender, delphinium, gaura, mint, lemon thyme, lemon grass, bay laurel, tarra-

*gon, basil, feverfew, artichokes. This much I can
see with my eyes closed. Also: the big yellow and
white poppies in the bed on the south wall.*

*"You may have stayed at the Savoy, but I doubt
very much you stayed at the Savoy and lost sixteen thousand pounds at Annabel's."*

*I have eaten dinner on Super Bowl Sunday in the
most expensive restaurants in Detroit, Atlanta,
San Diego and Tampa Bay.*

*Interview in LAT with someone who just resur-
faced after thirteen years underground: "I never
defined myself as a fugitive. I defined myself as a
human being. Human beings have things they
have to deal with. Because I was Weather Underground, being a fugitive was something I had to
deal with, but it wasn't a definition of me." What
mean??? If a fugitive is what you are, how does it
change the situation to define yourself as a "human being"?*

*I fled Him down the nights and down the days
I fled Him down the arches of the years*

*The most terrifying verse I know: merrily merrily
merrily life is but a dream.*

DREAM, the next two entries nonetheless begin.

*I go to my mother's house in Laguna, crying.
Ward's daughter Belinda is also there. Catherine*

has been kidnapped, I tell my mother. "I thought she came to tell you she was having Christmas dinner at Chasen's," Belinda says.

A party in a house that seems to be this one. Wynn and Catherine and I live in it but so do my mother and father. The party is in progress and I go out on the beach for a little quiet. When I come back my father is waiting at the bottom of the stairs. Catherine is either drunk or drugged, he says. He can hear her vomiting upstairs but doesn't want to intrude. I run up and notice that the upstairs has been painted. This is a little disturbing: how much time exactly has passed?

The last entry in this notebook, not a dream, was actually not one but six notes, each made in a different pen and on a different page but all apparently made in response to the daily regimen Catherine had described in her eighth-grade autobiographical essay as "radiation zapping following the exsishun [*sic*] of a stage 1 good prognose [*sic*] breast lesion":

The linear accelerator, the mevatron, the bevatron.
"Just ask for R.O., it's in the tunnel."

"A week before you finish you'll go on the mevatron to get your electrons. Now you're getting your photons."
Photons? Or "protons"???

Waiting for the beam after the technician goes and the laser light finds the place.

The sensation of vibration when the beam comes.
The stunning silent bombardment, the entire elec-
tromagnetic field rearranged.

"You don't feel anything," Arnie Stine said. "The
beam doesn't feel like anything."
"Just between us nobody who hasn't been on that
table has any idea what the beam feels like," the
technician said.

The beam is my alpha and my omega

I finished this morning
How I feel is excluded, banished, deprived of the
beam
Alcestis, back from the tunnel and half in love
with death

3

Of course we would not need those last six notes to know what Elena's dreams were about.

Elena's dreams were about dying.

Elena's dreams were about getting old.

Nobody here has not had (will not have) Elena's dreams.

We all know that.

The point is that Elena didn't.

The point is that Elena remained remote most of all to herself, a clandestine agent who had so successfully compartmentalized her operation as to have lost access to her own cut-outs.

The last entry in this notebook is dated *April 27 1982*.

It would have been not quite four months later, August 1982, when Elena McMahon left Wynn Janklow.

Relocated to the East Coast, as she put it.

It would have been some three months after that, late November 1982, when she returned for the first time to California.

She had flown out from Washington on the morning flight to interview a Czech dissident then teaching at

UCLA and rumored to be short-listed for a Nobel Prize in literature. She had meant to do the interview and go straight to the airport and turn in the rental car and take the next flight back, but when she left UCLA she had driven not to the airport but up the Pacific Coast Highway. Just as she would make no conscious decision to walk off the 1984 campaign, just as she would make no conscious decision to ask for a flight to Miami instead of to Washington, she had made no conscious decision to do this. She was unaware even that the decision had been made until she found herself parking the rental car in the lot outside the market where she used to shop. She had gone into the drug-store and said hello to the pharmacist and picked up a couple of surfing magazines for Catherine and a jar of aloe gel for herself, a kind she had been unable to locate in Washington. The pharmacist asked if she had been away, he hadn't seen her in a while. She said that she had been away, yes. She said the same thing to the checkout clerk in the market, where she bought corn tortillas and serrano chiles, something else she had been unable to locate in Washington.

She had been away, yes.

Always good to get back, right.

With weather this dry they were lucky to have gotten through Thanksgiving without a fire, yes.

No way she was ready to start dealing with Christmas, no.

She had sat then in the rental car in the parking lot, almost deserted at four in the afternoon. Four in the afternoon was not the time of day when women who lived here shopped. Women who lived here shopped in the morning, before tennis, after working out. If she still lived here she would not be sitting in a rental car in the parking lot at four in the afternoon. One of the high school boys who worked in the market after school was stringing Christmas lights on the board advertising the day's specials. Another was rounding up carts, jamming the carts into long trains and propelling each train into the rack with a single extended finger. By the time the last light dropped behind Point Dume the carts were all racked and the Christmas lights were blinking red and green and she had stopped crying.

"What was that about," Treat Morrison said when she mentioned this to him.

"It was about my not belonging there anymore," she said.

"Where did you ever belong," Treat Morrison said.

Let me clarify something.

When I said that Elena McMahon and Treat Morrison were equally remote I was shortcutting, jumping ahead to the core dislocation in the personality, overlooking the clearly different ways in which each had learned to deal with that dislocation.

Elena's apparently impenetrable performances in the various roles assigned her were achieved (I see now) only with considerable effort and at considerable cost. All that reinvention, all those fast walks and clean starts, all that had cost something. It had cost something to grow up watching her father come and go and do his deals without ever noticing what it was he dealt. *Father's Occupation: Investor.* It had cost something to talk to Melissa Simon on Westlake Career Day when all her attention was focused on the beam. *You don't feel anything,* Arnie Stine said. *The beam doesn't feel like anything. Just between us nobody who hasn't been on that table has any idea what the beam feels like,* the technician said. It had cost something to remember the Fourth of July her father's friend brought fireworks up from the border and to confine the picture to the fat little sizzler rockets she had not liked and the sparklers that made fireflies in the hot desert twilight.

To limit what she heard to *half a margarita and I'm already flying, who needs the goombahs, we got our own show right here.*

To keep the name of her father's friend just outside the frame of what she remembered.

Of course the name of her father's friend was Max Epperson.

You knew it was.

Treat Morrison would not have needed to forget that detail.

Treat Morrison had built an entire career on remembering the details that might turn out to be wild cards, using them, playing them, sensing the opening and pressing the advantage. Unlike Elena, he had mastered his role, internalized it, perfected the performance until it betrayed no hint of the total disinterest at its core. He knew how to talk and he knew how to listen. He was widely assumed because he refused the use of translators to have a gift for languages, but in fact he communicated with nothing more than a kind of improvisational pidgin and very attentive listening. He could listen attentively in several languages, not excluding his own. Treat Morrison could listen attentively to a discussion in Tagalog about trade relations between the United States and Asia, and Treat Morrison could listen with the same exact calibration of attentiveness to a Houston bartender explaining how when the oil boom went belly up he zeroed in on bartending as an entrée to the private service sector. Once on the shuttle I sat across the aisle from Treat Morrison and watched him spend the entire flight, National to La Guardia, listening attentively to the stratagems employed by his seatmate in the course of commuting between his home in New Jersey and his office in Santa Ana.

"You have the Delta through Salt Lake," I heard Treat Morrison prompt when the conversation showed signs of lagging.

"Actually I prefer the American through Dallas," the seatmate said, confidence restored in the intrinsic interest of his subject.

"The American out of Newark."

"Out of Newark, sure, except Newark has the short runways, so when the weather goes, scratch Newark."

During the ride in from La Guardia I had asked Treat Morrison how he happened to have the Delta through Salt Lake at his fingertips.

"He'd already mentioned it," Treat Morrison said. "Before we were off the ground at National. He took it last week and hit some pretty hairy turbulence over the Wasatch Range. I listen. That's my business. Listening. That's the difference between me and the Harvard guys. The Harvard guys don't listen."

I had heard before about "the Harvard guys," also about "the guys who know how not to rattle their teacups" and "the guys with the killer serves and not too much else." This was a vein in Treat Morrison that would surface only when exhaustion or a drink or two had lowered his guard, and remained the only visible suggestion of whatever it had meant to him to come out of the West and confront the established world.

This was another area he was not inclined to explore.

"What the hell, the last I heard this was still one country," was what he said when I tried to pursue it. "Unless you people in the media have new information to the contrary."

He regarded me in truculent silence for a full thirty seconds, then seemed to remember that truculent silence was not his most productive tack.

"Here's the deal," he said. "There are two kinds of people who end up in the State Department. And believe me, I am by *no means* talking about where somebody came from, I'm talking about what kind of person he is."

He hesitated.

A quick glance to assess my reaction, then the amendment: "And of course I mean what kind of person *he is or she is*. Male, female, space alien, whatever. I don't want to read some PC crap about myself in the goddamn New York *Times*. Okay. State. Two kinds of individuals end up there. There's the kind of individual who goes from post to post getting the place cards right and sending out the reminder cards on time. And there's the other kind. I'm one of the other kind."

I asked what kind that was.

"Crisis junkies," he said. "I'm in this for the buzz, take it or leave it."

This was Treat Morrison when his performance went off. When it was on he was flawless, talking as attentively as he listened, rendering opinions, offering advice, even volunteering surprisingly candid analyses of his own modus operandi. "There's a trick to inserting yourself in a certain kind of situation," he said when I once remarked on his ability to move from end game to end game without becoming inconveniently identified with any of them. "You can't go all the way with it. You have to go back and write the report or whatever, give the briefings, then move on. You go in, you pull their irons out of the fire, you get a free period, maybe six months, no more, during which you're allowed to lecture everybody who isn't up to speed on this one little problem on the frivolity of whatever other damn thing they've been doing. After that you move past it. You know who the unreported casualties of Vietnam were? Reporters and policy guys who didn't move past it."

That was another difference between Treat Morrison and Elena.

Elena inserted herself in a certain kind of situation and went all the way with it.

Elena failed to move past it.

Which is why, by the time Treat Morrison arrived on the scene, Elena had already been caught in the pipeline, swept into the conduits.

Into the game.

Into the plot.

Into the setup.

Into whatever you wanted to call it.

Four

Four

I

O ne of the many questions that several teams of congressional investigators and Rand Corporation analysts would eventually fail to resolve was why, by the time Treat Morrison arrived on the island, almost six weeks after she had learned from the Miami *Herald* that her father was dead and more than a month after she had learned from the FBI that the passport she was using had a trick built into it, Elena McMahon was still there.

She could have left.

Just gone to the airport and gotten on a plane (there were still scheduled flights, not as many as there had been but the airport was open) and left the place.

She would have known since the initial FBI interview that the passport with the trick built into it would not be valid for reentry into the United States, but that in itself might well have seemed an argument to get off this island, go somewhere else, go anywhere else.

She had some cash, there were places she could have gone.

Just look at a map: unnumbered other islands there

in the palest-blue shallows of the Caribbean, careless islands with careless immigration controls, islands with no designated role in what was going on down there.

Islands on which nothing either overt or covert was under way, islands on which the U.S. Department of State had not yet had occasion to place repeated travel advisories, islands on which the resident U.S. government officials had not yet found it necessary to send out their own dependents and nonessential personnel.

Islands on which the ranking American diplomatic officer was not said to be targeted for assassination.

Entire archipelagoes of neutral havens where an American woman of a certain appearance could have got off the plane and checked into a promising resort hotel (a promising resort hotel would be defined as one in which there were no Special Forces in the lobby, no armored unmarked vans at the main entrance) and ordered a cold drink and dialed a familiar number in Century City or Malibu and let Wynn Janklow and the concierge work out the logistics of reentry into her previous life.

Just think about it: this was not a woman who on the evidence had ever lacked the resources to just get on a plane and leave.

So why hadn't she.

The Rand analysts, I believe because they sensed the possibility of reaching an answer better left on the horizon, allowed this question to remain open, one of several "still vexing areas left to be further explored by future students of this period." The congressional investigators answered the question like the prosecutors many of them had been, resorting to one of those doubtful scenarios that tend to bypass recognizable human behavior in the rush to prove "motive." The motive on which the congressional investigators would settle in this instance was "greed": CAUGHT BY GREED, the pertinent section heading reads in their final report. Elena McMahon, they concluded, had stayed on the island because she still expected someone to walk up and hand her the million dollars she was supposed to have received on delivery of Dick McMahon's last shipment.

"Elena McMahon stayed where she was," to quote this section exactly, "because she apparently feared that if she left she would be cheated out of or would otherwise forfeit the money she believed she was owed, i.e., the payment she claimed was due her father."

But that was flat wrong.

The payment due her father was by then no longer the point.

The payment due her father had stopped being the point at the instant she read in the Miami *Herald* that her father had been certified dead at the Clearview Convalescent Lodge in South Kendall on June 30 1984.

Which happened also to be the date on the passport with the trick built into it.

My understanding is that Dick McMahon will not be a problem.

2

"Stop talking to the goddamn baby-sitter," her father had said the evening she was about to leave the house in Sweetwater for Fort Lauderdale–Hollywood International Airport and the unscheduled flight that would not land in San José, Costa Rica.

She was trying to tell the nurse about her father's midnight medication.

"Ellie. I want you to listen to me."

"He won't swallow it but you can mash it up in a little brandy," she said to the nurse.

The nurse continued flicking through channels.

"Don't let any of those guys talk you into staying over down there," her father said. "You deliver the goods, you pick up the payment, you get back on the plane, you're back here tomorrow. That's my deal."

"I thought *Cheers* was on two," the nurse said.

"Get the TV critic out of here and listen to me," Dick McMahon said.

She sent the nurse to locate *Cheers* in the kitchen.

"That one's not really a nurse," Dick McMahon said. "The one in the morning, she's a nurse, but that one's a baby-sitter." He had leaned back in his chair, exhausted. "Ellie. Okay. You deliver the goods, you pick up the payment, you get back on the plane. That's my deal." Each time he said this it was as if for the first time. "Don't let any of those guys mickey-mouse you into staying over, you follow me?"

She said that she followed him.

"Anybody gives you any trouble, you just tell them."

She waited.

She could see the network of veins beneath the transparent skin of his eyelids.

Tell them what, she prompted.

"Tell them, oh *goddamn*." He was rousing himself with difficulty. "Tell them they're going to have to answer to Max Epperson. Then you call Max. Promise me you'll call Max."

She did not know whether Max Epperson was dead or alive or a hallucination but she promised nonetheless that she would call Max.

Wherever Max might be.

"You just tell Max I'm a little under the weather," Dick McMahon said. "Tell Max I need him to look out for you. Just until I'm a hundred percent again. Just tell him I said that, you understand?"

She said that she understood.

Barry Sedlow had told her to be at Fort Lauderdale–Hollywood at midnight sharp.

She was to wait not in the terminal but at Post J, if she asked at the Butler operations office they would direct her to Post J.

At Post J there would be a locked gate onto the tarmac.

She was to wait at Post J.

Someone would unlock the gate.

By the time she was ready to leave her father was again asleep in his chair, but when she kissed his forehead he reached for her hand.

"You don't remember this but when you had your tonsils out I wouldn't let you stay in the hospital by yourself," he said. "I was afraid you'd wake up scared with nobody around. So I slept in a chair in your room."

Elena did not remember this.

All Elena remembered was that when Catherine had appendicitis she herself had slept on a gurney in Catherine's room at Cedars.

Her father's eyes were still closed.

He did not let go of her hand.

These were the next-to-last words her father spoke to her:

"You never even knew that, see. Because you were a winner, you took the whole hospital deal like a winner, you didn't wake up once."

"I did wake up," she said. "I do remember."

She wished she did.

She hoped Catherine would.

She held his hand until his breathing was even, then walked to the door.

"This payday comes in," he said when she opened the screen door, "for the first time in my life I'll have something to leave you."

"I did wake up," she repeated. "I knew you were there."

By the way.

I saw your dad.

He says hi.
I'm keeping him in the picture.

In fact I know why Elena McMahon was still on the island.

Elena McMahon was still on the island because of what she had known since the instant she read in the Miami *Herald* that her father had been certified dead in South Kendall on the same day the passport with her photograph on it was supposed to have been issued in Miami. What she had known since that instant was this:

Somebody out there was playing a different game, doing a different deal.

Not her father's deal.

A deal her father had not known about.

Her father's role in this deal he had not known about was to have been something more than just assembling the shipments, the shipments that had over the course of the spring refocused his dwindling energy, his flagging interest in staying alive. Her father's role was to have begun once he arrived on the ground to collect the million-dollar payday.

Consider her father: a half-crazy old man who had spent his life dealing merchandise that nobody would admit they wanted dealt, an old man whose interest in who used his merchandise was limited to who could pay for it, an old man whose well-documented impartiality about where his merchandise ended up could allow him to be placed on the wrong side of whatever was going to happen on this island.

Who would miss him, who would care?

Who would not believe he had done whatever it was they were going to say he had done?

An old man in a sick season.

An old man with no reputation to lose.

The shipments had just been the cheese in the trap.

She had sprung the trap and her father was dead and now she was set up to do whatever it was that he was supposed to have done.

Somebody had her lined up, somebody had her jacked in the headlights.

Had her in the scope.

Had her in the crosshairs.

What she did not know was who.

And until she knew who, until she located the line of fire, she could not involve Wynn.

She needed Wynn out of the line of fire.

She needed Wynn to take care of Catherine.

3

The question of why Treat Morrison arrived on the island was another area in which neither Rand nor the congressional investigators did a particularly convincing job, but in this case there would have been daunting structural obstacles, entire layers of bureaucracy dedicated to the principle that self-perpetuation depended on the ability not to elucidate but to obscure. "The cooperation of those individuals and agencies who responded to our numerous requests is appreciated," the preface to the Rand study noted in this connection. "Although some other individuals and agencies did not acknowledge or respond to our requests, it is to be hoped that future assessments of this incident will benefit from their assistance and clarification."

I also knew at the time why Treat Morrison arrived on the island, but it was not an answer calculated to satisfy the Rand analysts.

Treat Morrison arrived on the island for the buzz.

The action, the play.

Treat Morrison arrived on the island because it was

one more place where he could insert himself into a certain kind of situation.

Of course he had a "mission," a specific charter, and he also had a specific agenda. He always had a specific mission when he inserted himself into this kind of situation, and he also always had a specific agenda. The agenda did not necessarily coincide with the charter, but neither did it, if the insertion was smooth, necessarily conflict. "Certain people in Washington might have certain front-burner interests they want me to address, and that would be my charter," he once told me to this point, his tone that of someone explaining to a child what goes on at the office. "Typically, however, there might be some other little angle, something they maybe don't know about or think is back-burner. And I might also try to address that."

That would be his agenda.

Treat Morrison's charter in this case was to correct or clarify whatever misunderstandings or erroneous impressions might or might not have been left during the recent tour of the region undertaken by a certain senator and his senior foreign policy aide. There had then been a subsequent trip, made by only the senior foreign policy aide, who was twenty-seven years old and whose name was Mark Berquist. Various questions had been raised, by American embassy personnel in the countries involved, having to do with what the senator and Mark Berquist were doing in these countries and with whom they had been meeting and what, during such meetings, had been said or not said. These questions, which of course derived from a general suspicion that the visits may have lent encouragement if not outright support to what were usually called "unauthorized fringe elements," had languished awhile on the Caribbean and Central American desks and then, once it seemed clear that no answers would be forthcoming, had been strategically leaked out of Tegucigalpa to the ranking American reporters who covered the area.

"According to well-placed embassy sources," was the way the New York *Times* had attributed the questions.

The Los Angeles *Times* had added corroboration from "a European diplomat experienced in the region."

The Washington *Post* had relied on "knowledgeable U.S. observers."

In the brief flurry that followed, Mark Berquist defined the purpose of his trips as "strictly fact-finding," "generally focused on business and agricultural matters" but "not in any area of particular interest to you."

The senator himself said that he had made the trip only to "encourage participation in what is getting to be in our state a very active and mutually beneficial sister-city program."

The call for a hearing died before it got to subcommittee.

Which might have been the end of it had the visits from the senator and Mark Berquist not been followed, at least in the area on which Alex Brokaw's embassy reported, by certain incidents, not major but nonetheless troubling, in that they tended to legitimize the "previously reliable source" who had in late June reported the existence of a plot to assassinate Alex Brokaw.

There had been for example the two steamer trunks apparently abandoned in a windward condominium that had been rented, at the time of Mark Berquist's second visit, by a young Costa Rican woman who had since disappeared, skipped out on the weekly rent. When the owner returned he found the steamer trunks, which he moved into the hallway to be opened and discarded. The trunks sat in the breezeway for ten or twelve days before the janitor got around to opening them. According to the police report on the incident the contents of the two trunks included twenty Galil semiautomatic assault rifles, two AK-47s, seventeen silencers, three walkie-talkies, three bags of ammunition, assorted explosives and detonators and electronic devices, four bulletproof vests, and two sets of scales. According to the embassy report on the incident the presence of the scales argued for a drug connection and rendered the incident not of immediate concern. The embassy report further concluded that the absent Costa Rican tenant was not an asset of any U.S. agency known to the embassy.

That the tenant (no longer absent, since her body had been subsequently found in a ravine off the Smugglers' Cove highway) was not an asset of any U.S. agency known to the embassy was one thing Treat Morrison doubted.

A few days after the business with the steamer trunks (but before the young woman's body turned up) there had been the incident outside the Intercon, within minutes of Alex Brokaw's scheduled speech at a chamber of commerce lunch in the Intercon ballroom. There had been a small crowd, a demonstration of sorts, having to do with the question of who was responsible for the precipitous loss of the tourist business. It was the contention of the demonstrators that the United States was responsible for the precipitous loss of the tourist business. It was the contention of the embassy, and this was the point to which Alex Brokaw had intended to address his remarks, that the loss of the tourist business would be more than compensated for by the economic benefits that would accrue not only to this island but to the entire Caribbean basin were the United States Congress to approve military aid to the Nicaraguan freedom fighters for fiscal year 1985.

Economic benefits that were even now accruing.

In anticipation.

In recognition of the fact that there was already, let us be perfectly up front on this point, a presence.

A covert presence, true.

But only in anticipation of overt.

This was the subtext of the message that Alex Brokaw, alone in the back seat of his reinforced car, had been attempting to condense to an index card as his driver inched through the demonstrators outside the Intercon toward the police barricade set up at the entrance. The actual text of the message he was committing to the index card was this: *Just ask your friends the merchants of Panama what the United States Southern Command has meant to them.*

"Actually a fairly feeble demo," the driver reported having heard Alex Brokaw say at the exact instant it began to happen, first the quick burst of semiautomatic fire, then, as the police closed in, the dull pops of the tear gas canisters.

"Nothing like a little tear gas to clear out the sinuses," is what Alex Brokaw recalled saying.

According to the police report on the incident, inquiries focused on two Hondurans registered until that morning at the airport Days Inn. According to the embassy report on the incident, the two missing Hondurans could not be located for questioning but were not assets of any U.S. agency known to the embassy.

That the two missing Hondurans were not assets of any U.S. agency known to the embassy was a second thing Treat Morrison doubted.

The third thing Treat Morrison doubted was more amorphous, and had to do with the "previously reliable source" who had in late June reported the existence of a plot to assassinate Alex Brokaw. There was from the outset something about this report that had struck many people in Washington and Miami as overly convenient, beginning with the fact that it coincided with the workup sessions on legislation providing military aid to the Nicaraguan freedom fighters for fiscal year 1985. The same people in Washington and Miami tended to dismiss these recent incidents as equally convenient, further support for the theory that Alex Brokaw, in an effort to lay the foundation for a full-scale overt buildup on the island, had himself put the assassination report into play and was now lending credibility to the report with further suggestions of American personnel under siege.

"Clouding his own pond" was what Alex Brokaw was said to be doing.

The consensus that Alex Brokaw was clouding his own pond had by late July reached critical mass, as had the colliding metaphors: the way in which Alex Brokaw was said to be clouding his own pond was by "playing the Reichstag card."

The problem with clouding your own pond by playing the Reichstag card was that you would have to be fairly dense to try it, since otherwise you would know that everybody would immediately assume you were clouding your own pond by playing the Reichstag card.

That Alex Brokaw was sufficiently dense to so cloud his own pond was the third thing Treat Morrison doubted, and to locate the point at which these doubts intersected would have been part of his agenda. The other part of his agenda would have had to do with the unexpected visit he received, the evening before leaving Washington, from the senior foreign policy aide to the senator whose visit to the area had raised the original questions.

"T.M., I'll only be on your screen for fifteen minutes," Mark Berquist had said when he materialized, pink-cheeked and wearing a seersucker suit, in Treat Morrison's office after the secretaries had left. The air-conditioning was off and the windows were open and Mark Berquist's shirt had appeared to be constricting his throat. "It might be wise if we got some air."

"Mr. Berquist," Treat Morrison had said. "Why not sit down."

A barely perceptible pause. "Actually I'd prefer we took a walk," Mark Berquist had said meaningfully, his eyes scanning the bookshelves as if a listening device might reveal itself disguised as a copy of *Foreign Affairs*.

"I wouldn't presume to take up your time."

There had been a silence.

Treat Morrison had looked at his desk clock.

"You've wasted two minutes, which leaves you thirteen," Treat Morrison said.

There had been another silence, then Mark Berquist

took off his seersucker jacket and arranged it on the back of a chair. When he finally sat down he avoided looking directly at Treat Morrison.

"Let me give you a little personal background," Mark Berquist said then.

He said that he had been on the Hill for five years, ever since graduating from Villanova. At Villanova, he said, it so happened that he had been fortunate enough to know the sons of several prominent Cuban exiles, and the sons as well of two ambassadors to Washington from that general area, namely Argentina and El Salvador. It had been these friendships, he said, that ultimately led to his commitment to do his humble best to level the playing field for democracy in the area.

Treat Morrison turned his desk clock to face Mark Berquist.

"Seven," he said.

"You're aware that we have an interest there." Mark Berquist was finally meeting Treat Morrison's eyes. "A kind of situation."

"I'd get to it fast if I were you."

"It may be a situation you're not going to want to get into."

Treat Morrison at first said nothing.

"Goddamn," he said then. "I have actually never heard anyone say something like that." In fact this was not true. Treat Morrison had been hearing people say things like that his entire adult life, but none of these people had been twenty-seven-year-old staff aides on the Hill. "Call me naive, but I would have thought you'd have to be an actor to say something like that."

Treat Morrison had leaned back and clasped his

hands behind his head. "Ever given any thought to doing some acting, Mr. Berquist? Going on the boards? Smell of the greasepaint, roar of the crowd?"

Mark Berquist said nothing as he stood up.

"Not all that different from politics," Treat Morrison said. He was now studying the ceiling, squinting slightly at the overhead light. "If you stop to analyze it. I assume you saw certain people down there."

Mark Berquist yanked his seersucker jacket off the back of the chair, biting off each word evenly. "It's an old boys' town here, and you're one of the old boys, so feel free to take any shot you want. I am just telling you that this is a puzzle with a lot of pieces you may not want to put together."

"One of the people I'm assuming you saw was Bob Weir."

"That's a fishing expedition," Mark Berquist said. "And I'm not biting."

Treat Morrison said nothing.

Bob Weir was the "previously reliable source" who had in late June reported the existence of the plot to assassinate Alex Brokaw.

"And just let me add one thing," Mark Berquist said. "You would be making a serious error in judgment if you were to try to crucify Bob Weir."

Treat Morrison had watched in silence as Mark Berquist jabbed his arms into the seersucker jacket in an attempt to find the sleeves.

"By the way," Treat Morrison said then. "For future reference. I'm not an old boy."

4

Actually I had met Bob Weir.

I had come across him two years before, in 1982, in San Salvador, where he was running not a restaurant but a discotheque, a dispirited place called Chez Roberto, eight tables and a sound system in a strip mall in the San Benito district. Within hours of arriving in San Salvador I had begun hearing the name Bob Weir mentioned, always guardedly: it seemed that he was an American with what was called an interesting history, an apparent gift for being in interesting places at interesting times. He happened for example to have been managing an export firm in Guatemala at the time Jacobo Arbenz was overthrown. He happened to have been managing a second export firm, in Managua, at the time the Somoza regime was overthrown. In San Salvador he was said to be particularly close to a distinctly bad actor named Colonel Álvaro García Steiner, who had received special training from the Argentinian military in domestic counterterrorism, at that time a local specialty.

In the absence of anything more constructive to do I stopped by Chez Roberto on several different evenings, hoping to talk to its proprietor. There were the usual armored Cherokee Chiefs in the parking area and the usual Salvadoran businessmen inside (I never saw anyone dancing at Chez Roberto, nor in fact did I ever see a woman) but on each of these evenings Bob Weir was said to be "out of the city" or engaged in "other business" or simply "not seeing anyone at the present time."

It was some days after my last visit to Chez Roberto when a man I did not know sat down across from me in the coffee shop at the Sheraton. He was carrying one of the small zippered leather purses that in San Salvador at that time suggested the presence of a 9mm Browning, and he was also carrying a sheaf of recent American newspapers, which he folded open on the table and began to scan, grease pencil in hand.

I continued eating my shrimp cocktail.

"I see we have the usual agitprop from your colleagues," he said, grease-penciling a story datelined San Salvador in the Miami *Herald*.

Some time passed.

I finished the shrimp cocktail and signaled for a check.

According to the clock over the cashier's desk the man had now been reading the newspapers at my table for eleven minutes.

"Maybe I misunderstood the situation," he said as I signed the check. "I was under the impression you'd been looking for Bob Weir."

I asked if he were Bob Weir.

"I could be," he said.

This pointlessly sinister encounter ended, as many such encounters in San Salvador at that time ended, inconclusively. Bob Weir said that he would be more than happy to talk to me about the country, specifically about its citizens, who were entrepreneurial to the core and wanted no part of any authoritarian imposition of order. Bob Weir also said that he would be more than happy to introduce me to some of these entrepreneurial citizens, but unfortunately the ones I mentioned, most specifically Colonel Álvaro García Steiner, were out of the city or engaged in other business or simply not seeing anyone at the present time.

Many people who ran into Bob Weir of course assumed that he was CIA.

I had no particular reason to doubt this, but neither did I have any particular reason to believe it.

All I knew for certain about Bob Weir was that when I looked at his face I did not see his face.

I saw a forensic photograph of his face.

I saw his throat cut ear to ear.

I mentioned this to a few people and we all agreed: whatever Bob Weir was playing, he was in over his head. Bob Weir was an expendable. That Bob Weir was still alive and doing business two years later, not just doing business but doing it in yet another interesting place at yet another interesting time, not just doing it in this interesting place at this interesting time but doing it as a "previously reliable source," remains evidence of how little any of us understood.

5

When Treat Morrison told me later about his unexpected visit from Mark Berquist he said that he had been a little distracted.

Otherwise, he said, he would have handled it differently.

Wouldn't have let the kid get under his skin.

Would have focused in on what the kid was actually saying.

Underneath the derring-do.

Underneath the kid talking like he was goddamn General Lansdale.

He had been a little distracted, he said, ever since Diane died.

Diane Morrison, 52, wife of, after a short illness.

Diane, he said, had been one of God's bright and beautiful creatures, and at some point during the month or two before she died he had begun having trouble focusing in, trouble concentrating.

Then of course she did die.

He had finally straightened out the shifts with the nurses and just like that, she died.

And after that of course there was certain obligatory stuff.

The usual obligatory financial and social stuff, you know what I mean.

Then nothing.

The nurses weren't there and neither was she.

And one night he came home and he didn't want dinner and he didn't want to go to bed and he just kept having another drink until it was near enough to dawn to swim a few laps and go to the office.

Hell of a bad night, obviously.

And when he got to the office that morning, he said, he realized he'd been on overload too long, it was time to get away for a few days, he'd even considered going to Rome by himself but he didn't see how he could spare the time, and the end result was that he spent about eleven months running on empty.

Eleven months being a little distracted.

As far as this visit from Mark Berquist went, in the first place the kid had caught him working late, trying to clear his desk so he could get the early flight down there, it was imperative that he get the early flight because Alex Brokaw was delaying his own weekly flight to San José in order to brief him in the secure room at the airport, so this had been a situation in which he was maybe even more distracted than usual.

You can certainly see that, he added.

I was not sure that I could.

He had not been so distracted that he neglected to enter into his office log, since the secretaries who normally kept his schedule were gone, the details of the meeting in his own painstaking hand:

Date: Monday August 13 1984.
Place: 2201 C Street, N.W.
Time: In 7:10 p.m./out 7:27 p.m.
Present: T.A.M. / Mark Berquist
Subject: Unscheduled visit, B. Weir, other
    topics.

"That was just clerical," Treat Morrison said when
I mentioned the log entry. "That wasn't concentrating, that was just reflex, that was me covering my ass
like the clerks do, if you spent any time in Washington you'd know this, you do your goddamn log on
autopilot."

He was cracking the knuckles of his right hand,
a tic.

"As far as I was concerned," he said, "this was just
another kid from the Hill with wacko ideas that any
sane person had to know wouldn't get to first base
outside the goddamn District of Columbia."

He fell silent.

"Christ," he said then. "I should have taken the
three or four days and gone to Rome."

Again he fell silent.

I tried to picture Treat Morrison in Rome.

In the single image that came to mind he was walking by himself on the Veneto, early evening, everybody
sitting out in front of the Excelsior as if it were still
1954, everybody except Treat Morrison.

Shoulders slightly hunched, gaze straight ahead.

Walking past the Excelsior as if he had someplace to go.

"Because the point is," he said, then stopped. When
he again spoke his voice was reasonable but he was

again cracking the knuckles of his right hand. "The point is, if I'd gone to Rome, this meeting never had to happen. Because I would have been back on my game before this dipshit kid ever got south of Dulles."

It was he who kept circling back to this meeting with Mark Berquist, worrying it, chipping at it, trying to accommodate his failure to fully appreciate that the central piece in the puzzle he might not want to put together had been right there in his office.

Mark Berquist.

Which went to the question, as Treat Morrison would elliptically put it in the four hundred and seventy-six pages he committed to the Bancroft Library, of whether policy should be based on what was said or believed or wished for by people sitting in climate-controlled rooms in Washington or New York or whether policy should be based on what was seen and reported by the people who were actually on the ground. He had been, he kept repeating, a little distracted.

Had he not been a little distracted, he would have put it together immediately that the report of the plot to assassinate Alex Brokaw had not originated, as Alex Brokaw believed it had, with the previously reliable source who passed it to the embassy. Nor had it originated, as most people in Washington believed it had, with Alex Brokaw.

The report of the plot to assassinate Alex Brokaw had of course originated in Washington.

With Mark Berquist.

Who had passed it to the previously reliable source.

Bob Weir.

Treat Morrison had been that close to it and he had blown it.

He had not been concentrating.

Had he been concentrating, everything else would have fallen into place.

I mean Christ, he said. This isn't rocket science. This is textbook stuff. A, B, C. One two three.

If you put an assassination plot into play you follow it with an assassination attempt. If you stage an assassination attempt you put somebody out front.

A front, an assassin.

A front with a suitable background.

A front who can be silenced in the assassination attempt.

The assassination attempt which would or would not fail, depending on exactly how unauthorized the fringe elements turn out to be.

A, B, C. One two three.

Night follows day.

Not rocket science.

Had he been concentrating he would have added it up. Or so he was still telling himself.

The very last time we spoke.

6

The rhythm common to plots dictates a lull, a period of suspension, a time of lying in wait, a certain number of hours or days or weeks so commonplace as to suggest that the thing might not play out, the ball might not drop. In fact the weeks between the day Elena McMahon learned that her father was dead and the day Treat Morrison arrived on the island seemed on the surface so commonplace that only a certain rigidity in her schedule might have suggested that Elena McMahon was waiting for anything at all. At exactly six-thirty, on each of the mornings before she left the Intercon, she turned on the television set in her room and watched the weather on CNN International: showers over Romania, a front over Chile, the United States reduced to a system of thunderstorms, the marine layer shallowing out over southern California, the world beyond this island turning not slowly but at an inexorable meteorological clip, an overview she found soothing.

The shallowing out of the marine layer over southern California meant that stratus over Malibu would burn off by noon.

Catherine could lie in the sun today.

At no later than ten minutes past seven on each of those mornings she put on a pair of shorts and a T-shirt and began to walk. She walked five miles, seven miles, ten, however long it took to fill two hours exactly. At no later than ten minutes past nine she had two cups of coffee and one papaya, no more. She spent the two hours between ten and noon downtown, not exactly shopping but allowing herself to be seen, establishing her presence. Her routine did not vary: at the revolving rack outside the big Rexall she would pause each day to inspect the unchanging selection of postcards. Three blocks further she would stop at the harbor, sit on the low wall above the docks and watch the loading or unloading of one or another interisland freighter. After the Rexall and the harbor she inspected the bookstore, the pastry shop, the posters outside the municipal office. Her favorite poster showed a red circle and diagonal slash superimposed on an anopheles mosquito, but no legend to explain how the ban was to be effected.

The afternoons were at first more problematic. For a couple of days she tried sitting out by the Intercon pool, but something about the empty chaises and the unbroken summer overcast, as well as about the occasional appearance of one or another of the Americans who now seemed billeted at the Intercon in force, had made her uneasy. On the third day, in a secondhand bookstore near the medical school, she found an Italian grammar and a used textbook called *General Medicine and Infectious Diseases*, and after that spent allotted hours of each afternoon teaching herself Italian (from two to four) and (between five and seven) the principles of diagnosis and treatment.

After she moved from the Intercon to the windward side of the island she had her job, such as it was: assistant manager at the Surfrider. By the time she was hired there was already not much left to do, but at least she had a desk to arrange, a domain to survey, certain invented duties. There were the menus to be made, the flowers to be arranged. There was the daily run to the airport, in one of the Surfrider's three battered jeeps, to pick up the papers and mail and drop packages for shipment. On the windward side she had not the Intercon pool with its empty chaises but the sea itself, the oppressive low roar of the surf breaking on the reef and the abrupt stillness at ebb and full tide and the relief of the wind that came up toward dawn, banging the shutters and blowing the curtains and drying the sheets that were by then drenched with sweat.

On the windward side she also had, once the last backpacker moved on, the available and entirely undemanding companionship of the Surfrider manager, an American named Paul Schuster who had first come to the islands as a Pan American steward and had metamorphosed into a raconteur of the tropics with a ready trove of stories about people he had known (he would not say who but she would recognize the names if he told her) and curiosities he had encountered (she would not believe the readiness with which inhibition got shed under the palm trees) and places he had operated on islands up and down the Caribbean.

There had been the guesthouse on Martinique, the discotheque in Gustavia. Great spots but not his kind of spot. His kind of spot had been the ultra-exclusive all-male guesthouse on St. Lucia, total luxe, ten perfect jewel-box suites, only the crème de la crème there, he would not say who but major operators on Wall Street, the hottest-of-the-hot motion picture agents and executives, *pas de* hustlers. His kind of spot had also been Haiti, but he got scared out of Haiti when dead chickens began showing up on the gate of the place he had there, the first and for all he cared to know the only first-rate gay bathhouse in Port-au-Prince.

He might not be the smartest nelly on the block but hey, when he saw a dead chicken he knew what it meant and when he saw a hint he knew how to take it.

Pas de poulet.

Pas de voodoo.

Pas de Port-au-Prince.

Paul Schuster made frequent reference to his own and other people's homosexuality, but during the time Elena had been at the Surfrider there had been what might have seemed in retrospect a slightly off-key absence of evidence of this, no special friend, no boys who came or went, in fact no one who came or went or stayed, only the two of them, alone at meals and in the evening hours when they sat out by the drained pool and burned citronella sticks against the mosquitoes. Until the night before Treat Morrison arrived, Paul Schuster had been unflaggingly convivial, in a curiously dated style, as if he had washed up down here in the vicinity of 1952 and remained uncontaminated by the intervening decades.

"Happy hour," he would cry, materializing with a pitcher of rum punch on a porch where she was reading *General Medicine and Infectious Diseases.* "Chug-a-lug. Party time."

She would reluctantly mark her place and set aside *General Medicine and Infectious Diseases.*

Paul Schuster would again describe the scheme he had to redecorate and remarket the Surfrider as an ultra-luxe spa for European businessmen.

Top guys. Heavy hitters. Men of a certain class who may not be able to find full relaxation in Düsseldorf or wherever.

She would again say that she was not at all certain that the mood on the island at this very moment exactly lent itself to remarketing the Surfrider.

He would again ignore this.

"Here I go again," he would say. "Spilling my ideas like seed." This was a simile that never failed to please him. "Spilling my seed out where anybody in the world can lap it up. But hey, ideas are like buses, anybody can take one."

The one evening Paul Schuster was not unflaggingly convivial was that of August 13, which happened also to be the one evening he had invited a guest to dinner.

"By the way, I told Evelina we'll be three tonight," he had said when she came back from her morning trip to the airport. Evelina was the one remaining member of the kitchen staff, a dour woman who more or less stayed on because she and her grandchildren lived rent-free in a cottage behind the laundry. "I have a chum coming by, somebody you should know."

She had asked who.

"Kind of a famous restaurateur here," Paul Schuster had said.

When she came downstairs not long after seven Elena could see Paul Schuster and an older man sitting outside by the empty pool, but because the two seemed locked in intense conversation she picked up a magazine on the screened porch, where Evelina was already setting the table.

"Stop hiding in there." Paul Schuster's voice was imperious. "I want you to meet our guest."

As she walked outside the older man had half risen, the barest gesture, then sunk back into his chair, a rather ghostly apparition in espadrilles and unpressed khaki pants and a black silk shirt buttoned up to the neck.

"*Enchanté*," he had murmured, in a gravelly but clearly American accent. "Bob Weir."

"I'm frankly surprised you haven't run into Bob before," Paul Schuster said, a slight edge in his voice. "Bob makes it his business to run into everybody. That's how he could turn up here one morning and by dinner he's the best-known American on the island." Paul Schuster snapped his fingers. "He was at it before he even cleared customs. Running into people. Wouldn't you say that was the secret of your success, Bob?"

"Make your point, don't do it the hard way," Bob Weir said.

In the silence that followed, Elena had heard herself asking Bob Weir how long he had been here.

He had considered this. "A while now," he said finally.

There was another silence.

She was about to ask him about his restaurant when he suddenly spoke. "I believe I saw you at the airport this morning," he said.

She said that she was at the airport every morning.

"That's good," Bob Weir said.

This enigmatic pronouncement hung in the air between them.

She noticed that Paul Schuster was leaning slightly forward, tensed, transfixed.

"I don't know that it's *good* exactly," she said finally, trying for a little silvery laugh, a Westlake Mom tone. "It's just part of my job."

"It's good," Bob Weir said. "Because you can take Paul with you tomorrow. Paul has something to do at the airport tomorrow morning."

"Oh no I don't," Paul Schuster said. It seemed to Elena that he had physically recoiled. "Uh uh. I don't go to the airport."

"At ten." Bob Weir addressed this to Elena as if Paul Schuster had not spoken. "Paul needs to be there at ten."

"I do *not* need to be there at ten," Paul Schuster said.

"We can be there whenever you want," Elena said, conciliatory.

"Paul needs to be there at ten," Bob Weir repeated.

"Let me just lay one or two home truths on the table," Paul Schuster said to Bob Weir. "*Paul* doesn't need to be there at all. *She'll* be there if and when I tell her to be there. And believe me, there's still a big *if* in this situation, and the big *if* is *moi*." Paul Schuster snatched up the empty pitcher of rum punch. "And *if* she's there, you know who'll be there with her? Nobody. *Nul.* Period. Now let's just change the subject. We're out of punch. Get Evelina out here."

Elena stood up and started toward the porch.

"In my personal view you don't have as many home truths in your deck as you think you do," she heard Bob Weir say to Paul Schuster.

"What do I see on that porch," she heard Paul Schuster say, an accusation. "Do I see that Evelina has already set the table?"

Elena stopped. The hour at which dinner was served, meaning the hour at which Evelina would be free to go back to the cottage with her grandchildren, had become during the preceding week a minor irritation to Paul Schuster, but he had not before made an issue of it. It occurred to her that she could be witnessing some form of homosexual panic, that Bob Weir might know something that Paul Schuster did not want him to know.

"Evelina," he called. "Get out here."

Evelina had appeared, her face impassive.

"I sincerely hope you're not planning to foist dinner on us before eight-thirty exactly."

Evelina had stood there.

"And if you're about to tell me as usual the fish will dry out by eight-thirty," Paul Schuster said, "then let me cut this short. *Don't bring it out at all. Forget the fish. Pas de poisson.*"

Evelina's eyes flickered from Paul Schuster to Elena.

"Don't look to *her*," Paul Schuster said. "She just works here. She's just one of the help. Same as you used to be." Paul Schuster picked up the empty pitcher and handed it to Evelina. "If you would be good enough to refill this pitcher," he said as he started inside, "I'll call into town for the truck."

Evelina was halfway into the kitchen before she asked why the truck.

"Because I want you and your bastard brats out of here tonight," Paul Schuster said, and let the door bang behind him.

Elena closed her eyes and tried to breathe deeply enough to relax the knot in her stomach. She could hear Paul Schuster inside, singing snatches from

Carousel. In a locked rattan cabinet in his office he kept original-cast recordings of a number of Broadway musicals, worn LPs in mildewed sleeves, so scratched by now that he rarely played them but frequently sang them, particularly the lesser-known transitions, doing all the parts.

He's dead, Nettie, what am I going to do, she heard him ask, soprano.

He seemed to be in the vicinity of his office.

Why, you're going to stay here with me, she heard him answer himself, alto. *Main thing is to keep on living, keep on caring what's going to happen.*

He seemed now to be in the kitchen.

"Paul has a genuine theatrical flair," she heard Bob Weir say.

She said nothing.

" 'Neh-ver, no neh-ver, walk ah-lone,' " Paul Schuster was singing as he returned. He was carrying a full pitcher of punch. "All's well that ends well. We *dine* at eight-thirty."

"Maybe I should have mentioned this before," Bob Weir said. "I didn't come by to eat."

Elena said nothing.

"I've lived down here long enough to know," Paul Schuster had said. "Sometimes you have to take a strong position. Isn't that so, Elise?"

Elena said that she supposed it was so.

Paul Schuster picked up the pitcher of punch and filled his glass.

Elena said no more for me thank you.

Paul Schuster wheeled to face Elena. "Who asked you," he said.

"You're driving the cattle right through the fence," Bob Weir said to Paul Schuster.

"I think you must be stupid," Paul Schuster had said to Elena. He was standing over her, holding the pitcher of punch. "Are you stupid? Just how stupid are you? Are you stupid enough to just sit there while I do this?"

She looked up at him just in time to get the full stream of punch in her eyes.

"And since you're the one drove the cattle through it," she heard Bob Weir say to Paul Schuster, "you better goddamn well mend it."

She had gotten up, the sticky punch still running down her hair and face, her eyes stinging from the citrus, and walked into the empty hotel and up the stairs. That was the night she stood in the rusted bathtub and let the shower run over her for a full ten minutes, the drought and the empty cistern and the well going dry notwithstanding. That was also the night she called Catherine at the house in Malibu and told her that she would try to be home before school started.

"Home where," Catherine had asked, wary.

There had been a silence.

"Home wherever you are," Elena had said finally.

After she hung up she pulled a chair to the window and sat in the dark, looking out at the sea. At one point she heard raised voices downstairs, and then the sound of cars backing out the gravel driveway.

More than one car.

Two cars.

Paul Schuster was still downstairs, she could hear him.

Which meant that someone other than Bob Weir must have come by.

She told herself that Paul Schuster had been drinking and would apologize in the morning, that whatever the business about the airport had been it was something between him and Bob Weir and whoever else had arrived after she came upstairs, nothing to do with her, but when she woke in the morning she played back in her mind the sound of the raised voices. She had been listening the night before for Bob Weir's voice and she had been listening the night before for Paul Schuster's voice but only when she woke in the morning was she able to separate out a third voice.

My understanding is that Dick McMahon will not be a problem.

Transit passenger, not our deal.

It was when she separated out the voice of the Salvadoran that she understood that she would need to find someplace else to stay.

Someplace where the airport would not be an issue.

Whatever the issue was.

Someplace where the Salvadoran would not appear.

Someplace where she would not have to see Paul Schuster.

Someplace where he could not find out who she was.

At the time later that morning when Treat Morrison walked into the Intercon coffee shop and saw Elena McMahon sitting alone at the round table set for eight there remained a number of things she did not understand.

The first thing Elena McMahon did not understand was that Paul Schuster already knew who she was.

Paul Schuster had known all along who she was.

She was Dick McMahon's daughter.

She was who they had to front the deal since they did not have Dick McMahon.

Paul Schuster had known this ever since Bob Weir told him to hire her.

Told him to hire her and send her to the airport every morning.

Send her to the airport every morning to establish a pattern.

A pattern that would coincide with Alex Brokaw's weekly trips to San José.

Until now, Paul Schuster had always done what Bob Weir told him to do. The reason Paul Schuster had always done what Bob Weir told him to do (until now) was that Bob Weir had knowledge of certain minor drug deals in which Paul Schuster had been involved. This knowledge on Bob Weir's part had seemed to Paul Schuster more significant than it might have seemed because one of the federal agencies with which Bob Weir had a connection was the Drug Enforcement Administration.

However.

This knowledge was not in the end sufficiently significant to ensure that Paul Schuster would have gone to the airport with Elena McMahon on that particular morning.

And believe me, there's still a big if *in this situation, and the big* if *is moi.*

Paul Schuster might not be the smartest nelly on the block, but when he saw a hint he knew how to take it.

Pas de airport.

What had been meant to happen at the airport that

morning was something else Elena McMahon did not understand.

Treat Morrison understood more.

Treat Morrison understood for example that "Bob Weir" was the name used in this part of the world by a certain individual who, were he to reenter the United States, would face outstanding charges for exporting weapons in violation of five federal statutes. Treat Morrison also understood that this certain individual, whose actual name as entered in the charges against him was Max Epperson, could not in fact, for this and other reasons, reenter the United States.

What Treat Morrison understood was a good deal more than what Elena McMahon understood, but in the end Treat Morrison still did not understand enough. Treat Morrison did not for example understand that Max Epperson, also known as "Bob Weir," had in fact reentered the United States, and quite recently.

Max Epperson had reentered the United States by the process, actually not all that uncommon, known as "going in black," making prior covert arrangement to circumvent normal immigration procedures.

First in the early spring of 1984, and a second time in June of 1984, Max Epperson had reentered the United States without passing through immigration control, entering in the first instance via a military plane that landed at Homestead AFB and in the second via a commercial flight to Grand Cayman and a United States Coast Guard vessel into the Port of Miami. The first reentry had been for the express purpose of setting up a certain deal with a longtime partner.

The second reentry had been for the express purpose of confirming this deal.

Making sure that this deal would go down on schedule and as planned.

Ensuring that the execution of the deal would leave no window for variation from its intention.

Impressing the urgency of this on Dick McMahon.

Max Epperson's longtime partner.

Max Epperson's old friend.

Who needs the goombahs, we got our own show right here.

Max Epperson's backup in uncounted deals, including the ones on which he faced charges.

Somebody had to talk reason to Epperson, Dick McMahon had said to Elena the first morning at Jackson Memorial. *Epperson could queer the whole deal, Epperson was off the reservation, didn't know the first thing about the business he was in.*

It will have occurred to you that Max Epperson, in order to so reenter the United States, in order to go in black, necessarily had the cooperation of a federal agency authorized to conduct clandestine operations. As far as Treat Morrison went, it would have gone without saying that Max Epperson could have had the cooperation of a federal agency authorized to conduct clandestine operations. Max Epperson would naturally have been transformed, at the time the federal weapons charges were brought against him, into a professional informant, an asset for hire. The transformation of Max Epperson into the professional known as "Bob Weir" would have been the purpose in bringing the charges in the first place. This was an equation Treat Morrison, distracted or not distracted, could have done in his sleep. What Treat Morrison had

failed to figure was the extent to which his seeing
Elena McMahon in the Intercon coffee shop would
modify the equation.

She would still be the front, but Alex Brokaw would
no longer be the target.

I'm not sure I know what business Epperson is in,
she had said to her father that morning at Jackson
Memorial.

Christ, what business are they all in, her father had
said to her.

Five

Five

I

When I look back now on what happened I see mainly fragments, flashes, a momentary phantasmagoria in which everyone focused on some different aspect and nobody at all saw the whole.

I had been down there only two days when it happened.

Treat Morrison had not wanted me to come down at all.

I had told him before he left Washington that in order to write the piece I wanted to write it would be essential to see him in action, see him *in situ*, observe him inserting himself into a certain kind of situation. He had seemed at the time to concede the efficacy of such a visit, but any such concession had been, I realized quite soon, only in principle.

Only in the abstract.

Only until he got down there.

When I called to say that I was coming down he did not exactly put me off, but neither did he offer undue encouragement.

Actually it was turning out to be kind of a fluid situation, he said on the telephone.

Actually he wasn't certain how long he'd be there.

Actually if he was there at all, he was going to be pretty much tied up.

Actually we could talk a hell of a lot more productively in Washington.

I decided to break the impasse.

At that time I happened to own a few shares of Morrison Knudsen stock, and it had recently occurred to me, when I received an annual report mentioning Morrison Knudsen's role in a new landing facility under construction on the island, that this otherwise uninteresting island to which Treat Morrison had so abruptly decamped might be about to become a new Ilopango, a new Palmerola, a staging area for the next transformation of the war we were not fighting.

I looked at the clock, then asked Treat Morrison about the landing facility.

He was silent for exactly seven seconds, the length of time it took him to calculate that I would be more effectively managed if allowed to come down than left on my own reading annual reports.

But hell, he said then. It's your ticket, it's a free country, you do what you want.

What I did not know even after I got there was that the reason he had resisted my visit was in this instance not professional but personal. Because by seven o'clock on the evening of the day he arrived, although only certain people at the embassy knew it, Treat Morrison had managed to meet the woman he had seen eight hours before in the Intercon coffee shop. Two hours after that, he knew enough about her situation to place the call to Washington that got the DIA agent down in the morning.

That was the difference between him and the Harvard guys.

He listened.

2

I have no idea what was in her mind when she told him who she was.

Which she flat-out did. Volunteered it.

She was not Elise Meyer, she was Elena McMahon. She told him that within less than a minute after she went upstairs to his room with him that evening.

Maybe she recognized him from around Washington, maybe she thought he might recognize her from around Washington, maybe she had been feral too long, alert in the wild too long.

Maybe she just looked at him and she trusted him.

Because believe me, Elena McMahon had no particular reason, at that particular moment, to tell a perfect stranger, a perfect stranger who had *for reasons she did not know* approached her in the lobby of the Intercon, what she had not told anyone else.

I mean she had no idea in the world that had she gone to the airport at ten that morning Alex Brokaw would have been dead that night.

Of course Alex Brokaw was at the airport at ten, because he had delayed his weekly flight to San José in order to brief Treat Morrison.

Of course Alex Brokaw was still alive that night, because Dick McMahon's daughter had not been at the airport.

Of course.

We now know that, but she did not.

I mean she knew nothing.

She did not know that the Salvadoran whose voice she had most recently heard the night before trying to mediate whatever the argument had been between Paul Schuster and Bob Weir was Bob Weir's old friend from San Salvador, Colonel Álvaro García Steiner.

Deal me out, Paul Schuster had kept saying. *Just deal me out.*

You have a problem, Bob Weir had kept saying.

There is no problem, the Salvadoran had kept saying.

She did not even know that Paul Schuster had died that morning in his office at the Surfrider. According to the local police, who as it happened were now receiving the same training in counterterrorism from Colonel Álvaro García Steiner that Colonel Álvaro García Steiner had received from the Argentinians, there was no evidence that anyone else had been present in the office in the hours immediately preceding or following the death. Toxicological studies suggested an overdose of secobarbital.

It was late that first day, when he came back to the Intercon from the embassy, that Treat Morrison again noticed the woman he had seen that morning in the coffee shop.

He had been picking up his messages at the reception desk, about to go upstairs.

She had seemed to be pleading with the clerk, trying to get a room.

Nothing for you, the clerk had kept repeating. One hundred and ten percent booked.

I found a place I can move into tomorrow, she had kept repeating. I just need tonight. I just need a closet. I just need a rollaway in an office.

One hundred and ten percent booked.

Of course Treat Morrison intervened.

Of course he told the clerk to double up on one of the USG bookings, let him free up a room for her.

He had more than one reason to free up a USG room for her.

He had every reason to free up a USG room for her.

He already knew that she had arrived on the island on July 2 on an apparently falsified American passport issued in the name Elise Meyer. He had already been briefed on the progress of the continuing FBI investigation meant to ascertain who Elise Meyer was and what she was doing there. It went without saying that he would tell the clerk to free up a room for her. Just as it went without saying that he would suggest a drink in the bar while the clerk worked out the logistics.

She had ordered a Coca-Cola.

He had ordered an Early Times and soda.

She thanked him for his intervention.

She said that she had been staying in a place on the windward side and had been looking all day for a new place, but could not move into the place she wanted until the following day.

So she would be gone tomorrow.

She could promise him that.

No problem, he said.

She said nothing.

In fact she said nothing more until the drinks arrived, had seemed to retreat into herself in a way that reminded him of Diane.

Diane when she was sick.

Not Diane before.

When the drinks arrived she peeled the paper wrapping off a straw and stuck the straw between the ice cubes and, without ever lifting the glass from the table, drained half the Coca-Cola.

He watched this and found himself with nothing to say.

She looked at him.

"My father used to order Early Times," she said.

He asked if her father was alive.

There had been a silence then.

"I need to talk to you alone," she had said finally.

I told you.

I have no idea.

Maybe she told him who she was because he ordered Early Times. Maybe she looked at him and saw the fog off the Farallons, maybe he looked at her and saw the hot desert twilight. Maybe they looked at each other and knew that nothing they could do would matter as much as the slightest tremor of the earth, the blind trembling of the Pacific in its bowl, the heavy snows closing the mountain passes, the rattlers in the dry grass, the sharks cruising the deep cold water through the Golden Gate.

The seal's wide spindrift gaze toward paradise.

Oh yes.

This is a romance after all.

One more romance.

3

I recently tried to talk to Mark Berquist about what happened down there.

I know Mark Berquist slightly, everybody now knows Mark Berquist.

Youngest member of the youngest class ever elected to the United States Senate. The class that hit the ground running, the class that arrived on the Hill lean mean and good to go. Author of *Constitutional Coercion: Whose Rights Come First?* Maker of waves, reliable antagonist on the Sunday shows, most frequently requested speaker on the twenty-five-thousand-dollar-plus-full-expenses circuit.

Where his remarks were invariably distorted out of context by the media.

So invariably, his administrative aide advised me, that the senator was understandably wary about returning calls from the media.

"Wait just one minute," he said when I finally managed to waylay him, in the corridor outside a hearing, at a moment when the television crews who normally functioned as his protective shield had been temporarily diverted by a rumor that the President's wife had just entered the rotunda with Robert Redford. "I only speak to media on background."

I said that background was all I wanted.

I said that I was trying to get as much perspective as possible on a certain incident that had occurred in 1984.

Mark Berquist's eyes flickered suspiciously. Nineteen eighty-four had ended for him with the conclusion of that year's legislative session, and was as distant now as the Continental Congress. To bring up 1984 implied that the past had consequences, which *in situ* was not seen as a useful approach. This unspoken suggestion of consequences was in fact sufficiently unthinkable as to drive Mark Berquist to mount a broad-based defense.

"If this has anything to do with the period of the financing of the 1984 reelection campaign you can just file and forget," Mark Berquist said. "Since, and let me assure you that this is perfectly well documented, I didn't even move over to the executive branch until after the second inaugural."

I said that the period of the financing of the 1984 reelection campaign was not specifically the period I had in mind.

The period I had in mind was more the period of the resupply to the Nicaraguan contra forces.

"In the first place any reference to the so-called contra forces would be totally inaccurate," Mark Berquist said. "In the second place any reference to the so-called resupply would be totally inaccurate."

I suggested that both "contra" and "resupply" had become in the intervening years pretty much accepted usage for the forces and events in question.

"I would be extremely interested in seeing any

literature that used either term," Mark Berquist said.

I suggested that he could see such literature by having his staff call the Government Printing Office and ask for the February 1987 *Report of the President's Special Review Board*, the November 1987 *Report of the Congressional Committees Investigating the Iran-Contra Affair*, and the August 1993 *Final Report of the Independent Counsel for Iran/Contra Matters*.

There was a silence.

"These are matters about which there has already been quite enough misrepresentation and politicalization," Mark Berquist said then. "And to which I have no intention of contributing. However. Just let me say that anyone who uses the terms you used just betrays their ignorance, really. And to call it ignorance is putting the best face on it. Because it's something worse, really."

I asked what it really was.

"The cheapest kind of political bias. That's what the media never understood." He looked down the corridor as if for his missing press escort, then at his watch. "All right, one more shot. Your best question."

"On the record," I said, only reflexively, since whether it was on the record was of no real interest to me.

"Negative. No. You agreed to the ground rules. On background only."

The reason it was of no real interest to me whether this was on the record or on background was because Mark Berquist would never in his life tell me the one thing I wanted to know.

The one thing I wanted to know from Mark Berquist was not at what point the target had stopped being Alex Brokaw. I knew at what point the target had stopped being Alex Brokaw: the target had stopped being Alex Brokaw when Elena McMahon left the Surfrider, did not go to the airport, lost her potential proximity to Alex Brokaw. The one thing I wanted to know from Mark Berquist was at what point exactly *he had known* that the target had changed from Alex Brokaw to Treat Morrison.

I asked Mark Berquist this.

One shot, best question.

Mark Berquist's answer was this: "I can see you've bought hook, line and sinker into one of those sick conspiracy fantasies that, let me assure you, have been thoroughly and totally discredited and really, I mean time and time again. And again, calling this kind of smear job sick is putting the best face on it."

More colliding metaphors.

On background only.

4

It played out, when the time came, very quickly. For the last nine of the ten days he had been on the island they had been meeting at the place she had found, an anonymous locally owned motel, not a chain, the chains were by then fully booked for USG personnel, a two-story structure near the airport so unremarkable that you could have driven to the airport a dozen times a day and never noticed it was there.

The Aero Sands Beach Resort.

The Aero Sands was on a low bluff between the highway and the beach, not really a beach but a tidal flat on which some fill had been thrown to protect the eroding bluff. The bluff ended where the highway curved down to the water just south of the Aero Sands, but on the bluff a hundred or so yards north of the Aero Sands there was a small shopping center, a grocery and a liquor store and a video rental place and outlets for sports supplies and auto parts, and it was in the parking lot of this shopping center that Treat Morrison would leave his car.

He had checked all this out.

He did not want his car seen in the Aero Sands parking lot, he did not want to be seen himself entering the exposed front door of her room.

He wanted to approach the Aero Sands from where he could assess it, have ample time to pick up on any official presence, anyone who might recognize him, anything out of the ordinary.

On the first of the nine days Treat Morrison came to the Aero Sands he brought the DIA agent, who took her statement and flew directly back to Washington, airport to Aero Sands to airport, no contact with the embassy.

On the following days Treat Morrison came to the Aero Sands alone.

At a few minutes before whatever time he told her he would be there she would leave open the sliding glass back door to her room and walk across the concrete pool area behind the motel. From a certain point just past the small pool it was possible to look north and get a partial view of the path on the bluff, and she always did, hoping he might be early, but he never was. She would nod at the woman who every evening pushed both an old man in a wheelchair and a baby in a stroller around the pool. Then she would continue on, down the dozen rickety wooden steps to what passed for the beach. There in the clear, there in the open space between the water and the bluff, Elena McMahon would wait in a place where Treat Morrison could see her as he approached.

As he had told her to do.

The point was that he believed he was protecting her.

He believed this right up to the instant, at seven-twenty on the evening of the tenth day he had been on the island, a day in fact on which he had made the final arrangement to take her back to the United States with him, take her in black via DIA and get the whole goddamn situation worked out in Washington, when it happened.

After it was over, after the flight to Miami during which he had been mostly incoherent and after the surgery and after the ICU, at some point when he was alone in a private room at Jackson Memorial, Treat Morrison remembered passing the man on the bluff as he walked from the shopping center to where he could already see her on the beach.

There had been nothing out of the ordinary about seeing the man on the bluff.

Nothing at all.

Nothing about the man on the bluff to signal an official presence, nothing to suggest someone who by recognizing him could place her beyond his protection.

Nothing.

He had already been able to see her on the beach.

She had been wearing the same white dress she was wearing in the Intercon coffee shop.

She had been looking out across the tidal flat.

She had been watching the bioluminescence on the water out by the reef.

The man on the bluff had been leaning over, tying his shoe, his face obscured.

There was a full moon but the man's face had been obscured.

That the man's face had been obscured was of course something that did not occur to Treat Morrison until after the fact, by which time the man on the bluff was beside the point, since it had been immediately and incontrovertibly established, according to both the FBI and the local police, who had coincidentally been staking out the Aero Sands all that week on an unrelated drug matter, that the man on the bluff, if indeed there had been a man on the bluff, was not the would-be assassin.

The reason this had been immediately and incontrovertibly established was that the local police who had been so fortuitously on hand had managed to kill the would-be assassin right there on the beach, her white dress red with blood before her clip was even emptied.

What bothered Treat Morrison most was not just the man on the bluff.

What bothered him more, what had begun to bother him even as the anesthesiologist was telling him to count backward from one hundred, what was bothering him so much by the time he was alone in the private room at Jackson Memorial that the doctor ordered sedation added to his IV line, was that over the preceding nine days he had checked out the Aero Sands at many different times of day and night, from every possible angle and with every possible eventuality in mind, and he did not recall having at any point during that week seen the local police.

Who had been so fortuitously on hand.

Suggesting that they had not been there at all.

Suggesting that if they had been there at all they had been there only at a certain moment, only at the moment they were needed.

A conclusion that could lead nowhere, since Elena McMahon was already dead.

I mean you could add it up but where does it get you.

This was Treat Morrison's last word on the subject.

I mean it's not going to bring her back.

5

AMERICAN IMPLICATED IN ATTEMPTED ASSASSINA-
TION was the headline on the first AP story as
it ran in the Miami *Herald*, the only paper in which I
initially had occasion to see it. I recall reading it in
the elevator of the hospital where Treat Morrison had
finally been stabilized for the flight to Miami. It was
that morning's *Herald*, impossible to come by down
there except at the embassy, abandoned in the waiting
room by Alex Brokaw's DCM when the helicopter arrived to take Treat Morrison to the airport.

Colonel Álvaro García Steiner had also been in the
waiting room, watching warily from a sagging sofa as
the local police spokesman was interviewed by a San
Juan television channel.

The paper was lying on a molded plastic chair and
was folded open to this story.

As I picked it up I happened to look out the window
behind Colonel Álvaro García Steiner and see the helicopter, just lifting off the lawn.

I walked to the elevator and got on it and started to
read the story as the elevator descended.

The elevator had stopped to pick someone up on the

third floor when I hit the name of the American implicated in the attempted assassination.

Academy Award night, two and a half years before.

Was the last time I saw her.

Said to have been using the name Elise Meyer.

*Embassy sources confirmed however that her actual
name was Elena McMahon.*

*Reports that the suspected assassin had been sup-
plying arms and other aid to the Sandinista government in Nicaragua remain unconfirmed.*

Until the next day, when Bob Weir happened to find
himself in a position to provide the manifests that de-
tailed the shipments that happened to coincide with
weapons recently seized in a raid against a Sandinista
arms cache.

Also fortuitously.

Since the manifests confirmed the reports that the
suspected assassin had been supplying arms and other
aid to the Sandinista government in Nicaragua.

The reports that had been further corroborated by
the discovery of Sandinista literature in two adjoining
rooms at the Surfrider Hotel recently vacated by the
would-be assassin.

Immediately and incontrovertibly confirmed.

Immediately and incontrovertibly corroborated.

Which of course was the burden of the second
AP story.

6

Imagine how this went down.

She would have come out of the Aero Sands.

At the certain point just past the pool where it was possible to get a partial view of the path on the bluff she would have glanced up.

She would not have seen Treat Morrison.

She would have passed the woman who pushed the old man in the wheelchair and the baby in the stroller and she would have nodded at the three of them and the baby would have turned to look at her and the old man would have touched his hat and she would have reached the last of the rickety wooden steps onto the beach before she realized that there had been a man on the bluff and that she had seen the man before.

She would have not even consciously registered seeing the man on the bluff, she would have registered only that she had seen him before.

The man on the bluff with the ponytail.

The man at the landing strip in Costa Rica.

I could be overdue a night or two in Josie.

Anyone asks, tell them you're waiting for Mr. Jones.

You're *doing nothing. What* I'm *doing doesn't concern you.*

She had not registered seeing him but something about seeing him had slowed motion just perceptibly, twenty-four frames a second now reduced to twenty. The baby had turned too slowly.

As in the hour before our death.

The old man in the wheelchair had lifted his hand to his hat too slowly.

As in the hour before our death.

She did not want to look back but finally she did.

When she heard the shots.

When she saw Treat Morrison fall.

When she saw the man on the bluff turn to her.

You get it one way or you get it another, nobody comes through free.

7

After the two AP stories the story stopped, dropped into a vacuum.

No mention.

Off the screen.

That the intended political consequences never materialized was evidence, in retrospect, that Treat Morrison had not entirely lost his game.

"I mean it was just all wrong," he said to me. "It would have been just plain bad for the country."

I suggested that he had not done it for the country.

I suggested that he had done it for her.

He did not look directly at me. "It was just all wrong," he repeated.

Only once, a year or so later, did Treat Morrison almost break down.

Almost broke down in such a predictable way that I did not even bother recording what he said in my notes. I remember him talking again about being distracted and I remember him talking again about not concentrating and I recall him talking again about that dipshit kid never getting south of Dulles.

Goddamn, he kept saying.

You think you have it covered and you find out you don't have it covered worth a goddamn.

Because believe me this was just one hell of a bad outcome.

The last outcome you would have wanted.

If you'd been me in this deal.

Which of course you weren't.

So you have no real way of understanding.

I mean you could add it up but where does it get you.

I mean it's not going to bring her back.

So Treat Morrison told me.

The very last time we spoke.

8

Treat Morrison died four years later, at age fifty-nine, a cerebral hemorrhage on a ferry from Larnaca to Beirut. When I heard this I remembered a piece by J. Anthony Lukas in the New York *Times* about a conference, sponsored by the John F. Kennedy School of Government at Harvard, at which eight members of the Kennedy administration gathered at an old resort hotel in the Florida Keys to reassess the 1962 Cuban missile crisis.

The hotel was pink.

There was a winter storm off the Caribbean.

Theodore Sorensen swam with the dolphins. Robert McNamara expressed surprise that CINCSAC had sent out the DEFCON 2 alert instructions uncoded, in the clear, so that the Soviets would pick them up. Meetings were scheduled to leave afternoon hours for tennis doubles. Douglas Dillon and his wife and George Ball and his wife and McNamara and Arthur Schlesinger ate together by candlelight in the main dining room. Communications were received from Maxwell Taylor and Dean Rusk, too ill to attend.

When I read this piece I imagined the storm continuing.

The power failing, the tennis balls long since dead, the candles blowing out at the table in the main dining room where Douglas Dillon and his wife and George Ball and his wife and Robert McNamara and Arthur Schlesinger are sitting (not eating, no dinner has arrived, no dinner will arrive), the pale linen curtains in the main dining room blowing out, the rain on the parquet floor, the isolation, the excitement, the tropical storm.

Imperfect memories.

Time yet for a hundred indecisions.

A hundred visions and revisions.

When Treat Morrison died it occurred to me that I would like to have seen just such a reassessment of what he might have called (did in fact call) certain actions taken in 1984 in the matter of what later became known as the lethal, as opposed to the humanitarian, resupply.

Imperfect memories of the certain incident that should not have occurred and could not have been predicted.

By any quantitative measurement.

I would like to have seen such a reassessment take place at the same hotel in the Keys, the same weather, the same mangroves clattering, the same dolphins and the same tennis doubles, the same possibilities. I would like to have seen them all gathered there, old men in the tropics, old men in lime-colored pants and polo shirts and golf hats, old men at a pink hotel in a storm.

Of course Treat Morrison would have been there.

And when he went upstairs and opened the door to his room Elena McMahon would have been there.

Sitting on the balcony in her nightgown.

Watching the storm on the water.

And if you are about to say that if Elena McMahon was upstairs in this pink hotel there would have been no reason for the conference, no incident, no subject, no reason at all: *Just file and forget.*

As Mark Berquist would say.

Because of course Elena would have been there.

I want those two to have been together all their lives.

23 January 1996